The F

JOHN GRISHAM

Level 5

Retold by Robin Waterfield
Series Editors: Andy Hopkins and Jocelyn Potter

Pearson Education Limited
Edinburgh Gate, Harlow,
Essex CM20 2JE, England
and Associated Companies throughout the world.

ISBN: 978-1-4058-8243-9

The Firm © John Grisham 1991
First published in the United Kingdom by Century 1991
This adaptation first published by Penguin Books 1995
Published by Addison Wesley Longman Ltd and Penguin Books Ltd 1998
New edition first published 1999
This edition first published 2008

3 5 7 9 10 8 6 4 2

Text copyright © Robin Waterfield 1995
Illustrations copyright © Bob Harvey (Pennant Illustration Agency) 1995
All rights reserved

The moral right of the adapter and of the illustrator has been asserted

Typeset by Graphicraft Ltd, Hong Kong
Set in 11/14pt Bembo
Printed in China
SWTC/02

Published by Pearson Education Ltd in association with
Penguin Books Ltd, both companies being subsidiaries of Pearson Plc

For a complete list of the titles available in the Penguin Readers series please write to your local
Pearson Longman office or to: Penguin Readers Marketing Department, Pearson Education,
Edinburgh Gate, Harlow, Essex CM20 2JE, England.

Contents

Introduction

'I came here to meet you, and to warn you about the firm.'

'I'm listening,' Mitch said.

'Three things. First, don't trust anyone. Second, every word you say, at home or in the office, is probably being recorded.'

Mitch watched and listened carefully; Tarrance was enjoying this. 'And the third thing?' he asked.

'Money doesn't grow on trees.'

Although Mitch McDeere comes from a poor family, he has just graduated from Harvard Law School and he has a powerful desire to succeed. Young, handsome and intelligent, he wants it all: money, a big house and a fast car. He's climbing – and he wants to climb fast. So when he is offered a job at the super-rich law firm of Bendini, Lambert and Locke, he can hardly believe his luck. His wife, Abby, is also delighted. With the kind of money the firm has offered him, all their dreams can come true. But dreams come at a price.

The clients of Bendini, Lambert and Locke, in Memphis, Tennessee, are very rich. The firm's partners and associates frequently fly to the Cayman Islands in the Caribbean, where there are 300 banks, and 12,000 businesses have their head offices – at least on paper. It is a good place to hide money from the taxman. But the firm is hiding something much worse.

Mitch discovers that the FBI, the US Department of Justice's investigative branch, is watching the firm closely, and five of its members have died mysteriously. An FBI agent wants Mitch to help with their investigation. He has to decide: Is he going to risk his life and Abby's? Can he afford not to?

The Firm (1991) is John Grisham's second novel and was his first of many best-sellers. It sold over 12 million copies in paperback in the United States alone.

John Grisham was born in 1955 in Jonesboro, Arkansas, USA. His father was a building worker and the family were poor. They moved house frequently until 1967 when they settled in Southaven, Mississippi. Grisham's mother encouraged him to read when he was young, which began his love of books. He graduated in 1977 from Mississippi State University. From there he went to the University of Mississippi to study law, graduating in 1981. After graduating, he started his own law firm in Southaven. In 1983, he was elected to national government to represent the state of Mississippi, where he served until 1990. While working in politics, he continued his law practice.

In 1984, he started writing while working full-time. He got up at 5 a.m. each day so he could spend a few hours writing before going to the office. His first book, *A Time to Kill* (1989), did not sell well. It was about the tense atmosphere between blacks and whites in Clanton, Mississippi following a murder. Success soon followed with *The Firm* (1991), which was a number one best-seller. He sold it for $200,000 and the film rights for $600,000. He gave up his law work immediately and concentrated on writing. His third novel was *The Pelican Brief* (1992), and this made him world-famous. After that, he wrote one novel a year, and he became the world's best-selling novelist of the 1990s.

Grisham and his wife Renee have two children. They own a large farm in Mississippi and another near Charlottesville, Virginia. He earns well over $25 million a year from his books and from films of the books.

Grisham's knowledge of politics and the law plays a large part in his novels. The Mafia too is important in some of them, including this one. This secret crime society, which spread to the United States from Sicily in the late nineteenth century, is controlled by a few powerful families. The amount of power and control they have had over United States business and politics in some parts of the country is certainly dangerous. Making billions of dollars from illegal businesses, like drugs, the Mafia pours this money into legal businesses, which make even more profit. Fear and violence are easy weapons against anyone who talks to the police. For this reason, this Grisham story is not as unbelievable as it may seem.

Other novels by John Grisham include *The Client* (1993), about an eleven-year-old boy who discovers a hidden body. The FBI want him to tell them where it is. But the Mafia killers want to silence him. *The Chamber* (1994) tells the story of a man in prison on death row and a young lawyer who wants to help him. In *The Rainmaker* (1995), a young lawyer battles against some of the best lawyers that money can buy. In *The Partner* (1997), $90 million go missing from the law firm of a dead man. Then his partners learn that he is still very much alive. *The Testament* (1999) centres round a very rich man who is also very strange. In another story, three judges are sent to jail. They call themselves *The Brethren* (2000) and they carry on practising law until something goes very wrong. *The Innocent Man* (2006) is about a man who is wrongfully sent to prison in Oklahoma.

Many of Grisham's novels are available as Penguin Readers.

In 1993, *The Firm*, like many of Grisham's stories, was made into an exciting film. With a best-seller for a story and big names like Tom Cruise, Gene Hackman, and Holly Hunter, the film attracted large audiences round the world.

Chapter 1   Mitchell McDeere

Mitchell Y. McDeere was twenty-five years old. He was about to graduate in the top five from Harvard Law School. He had a beautiful wife, Abby. He was white, handsome, tall and physically fit. He didn't take drugs or drink too much. And he was hungry. He wanted it all: money, power, a big house, a fast car... He urgently wanted to succeed.

In other words, he was perfect for the Memphis law firm of Bendini, Lambert & Locke. Every one of the twenty partners in the firm was given a thick file on him. They knew that he had been born in poverty in Kentucky and brought up by his mother after his father's death. They knew that she had wasted the money the army gave her after her eldest son's death in Vietnam, and that only the other brother, Ray, had cared for him. They knew that he had won a place at Western Kentucky University because he was good at football, and had graduated top of his class. They could see the poverty hurt, and that he wanted to climb away from it.

Now he was about to leave Harvard. Two firms in New York and one in Chicago were interested in him, according to the file. The highest offer was $76,000 and the lowest was $68,000. All the partners agreed that he was the one they wanted. They needed a new associate this year and they wanted it to be him. The first interview, in a hotel near Harvard, went well. Oliver Lambert took with him Lamar Quin, an associate who had been with the firm for seven years, and offered Mitch $80,000, a new BMW and help in buying a house. Mitch was interested, of course. Lambert invited him down to Memphis to visit the firm. He said he would send the air tickets.

The figure of $80,000 started Mitch and Abby dreaming.

'Eighty thousand in Memphis is the same as one hundred and twenty thousand in New York,' Mitch said. 'We'll be able to afford almost anything we want. And it's only the money I'll *start* at: in two years I'll be into six figures. They say that on average an associate becomes a partner in about ten years, and then I'll be earning about half a million dollars a year! And what about the car and the house?'

'Who wants New York?' Abby said, smiling, and thinking about their rusty Mazda and about new furniture in a big old house – and dreaming of babies. 'What sort of work is it?'

'Taxes,' Mitch said, 'which is what I enjoy. And we both hate the cold weather in the north-east. The firm specializes in international tax law. Bendini started it in 1944. He had a lot of clients in the south, so he moved down to Memphis. And obviously everyone who works there loves it: they say that members very rarely leave the firm.'

'And you'd be closer to Ray.'

'True.'

'If they're offering so much, why doesn't everybody know about them and try to work there?'

'Lambert says they like to stay small. There are only forty-one members in all. They get one new member every two years, and they approach him rather than the other way round.'

'Why would they help us with a house?' Abby asked.

'It's important to the firm that their members stay happy and look rich. It helps to bring business in.'

'Memphis, here we come,' said Abby. 'I like this firm already.'

Chapter 2   Bendini, Lambert and Locke

Bendini had loved the firm's office building; he had also loved secrecy. Before his death in 1970 he had filled the 100-year-old building with electronic surveillance equipment, as well as with every luxury money could buy. Only a few special members could enter certain parts of the building.

In twenty years Bendini built the richest law firm in Memphis. It was also definitely the quietest. Every associate hired by the firm was taught the evils of a loose tongue. Everything was secret – especially clients' business. Young associates were warned that talking about the firm's business outside the firm could delay the prize of a partnership. Nothing left the building on Front Street. Wives were told not to ask questions – or were lied to. The associates were expected to work hard, keep quiet and spend their healthy incomes.

Lamar Quin met Mitch at the entrance to the building. After an embarrassing speech by Oliver Lambert in front of all the other associates in the second-floor library, Lamar took him on a tour of the office. There were excellent libraries on the first four floors of the five-floor building, so that no member needed to leave the office to find out anything.

The first four floors were almost the same. The centre of each floor was filled with secretaries, their desks and the necessary machines. On one side of the open area was the library and on the other were offices and smaller conference-rooms. Partners got the large corner offices, with wonderful views over the river and the city.

'You won't see any pretty secretaries,' Lamar said softly as they watched them work. 'These are the best legal secretaries in Memphis, but they also have to be over a certain age. The firm likes its members to have steady marriages. Babies are encouraged. Of course wives are not forbidden to work.'

'I hope not,' said Mitch, puzzled by the word 'forbidden'. He decided to change the subject. 'Does every lawyer get his own secretary?'

'Yes, until you're a partner. Then you'll get another, and by then you'll need one. Nathan Locke has three, all with twenty years' experience, and he keeps them busy. You'll find that the work takes at least eighty hours a week at first. And there's always more if you want it. Everyone works a hundred hours a week during tax season. We get well paid, all right, but we earn it, believe me.'

'What about holidays?'

'Two weeks a year for the first five years. I know that doesn't sound like very much, but the firm does own a couple of beach houses in the Cayman Islands, and you can usually get one for your holiday – as long as a partner doesn't want it, of course. We do a lot of business in the Caymans, as well, because the islands are tax-free. Nathan Locke's there at the moment, in fact, which is why you can't meet him today.'

Mitch had lunch with the partners in their special dining-room on the fifth floor. Again the generous public praise was embarrassing, but pleasing. Mitch wanted a beer to help him feel comfortable, but looking round he saw that no one had any alcohol, and he learned that drinking at lunch-time was not liked by the firm. Nor was heavy drinking at any time. They wanted members they could rely on. That was all right with Mitch. He was determined to succeed.

By the time Mitch left the building in the evening, after a meeting with Royce McKnight to discuss further details of his contract, he had decided: there could be no better offer in the whole country.

Chapter 3   The Fifth Floor

There were no law offices on the fifth floor of the Bendini Building. The partners' dining-room and kitchen filled the west end, then in the centre there were some empty rooms, and then there was a wall. In the centre of the wall was a small metal door with a button beside it and a camera over it. This opened on to a small room where an armed guard watched the door and studied a large number of television surveillance screens. A hall went past the offices and workrooms of a number of men whose job was to watch and to gather information. The windows to the outside world were painted over. DeVasher, the head of security, had the largest of these small, plain offices.

On the Monday after Mitch McDeere's visit, Oliver Lambert stood in front of the small metal door and stared at the camera over it. He pushed the button, waited and was finally allowed in. He walked quickly along the hall and entered DeVasher's office. They talked a bit about McDeere. DeVasher reported that, as far as he and his men could tell, Mitch would not be a security risk for the firm. He played Lambert a tape of phone calls from Mitch's hotel room in Memphis to Abby in Massachusetts.

'Very loving conversations, you see, Ollie,' DeVasher said with an evil grin on his face. 'They're just like a newly married couple. I'll try to get you some bedroom pictures later. I know how much you enjoy those. She is lovely.'

'Shut up, DeVasher,' Lambert said, and then, after a pause, 'I wish we could find his brother Ray. We know everything about his family, and hers, but we just can't find this brother.'

'Don't worry, Ollie,' DeVasher said. 'We'll find him.' DeVasher closed the McDeere file and opened another, much thicker one.

Lambert stared at the floor. 'What's the latest?' he asked softly.

'It's not good news, Ollie. Kozinski and Hodge are definitely working together now. Last week the FBI checked Kozinski's house and found our bugs.* Kozinski told Hodge when they were hiding in the third-floor library. Now they think everything's bugged and they're very careful where they talk.'

* *Bug*: a small hidden microphone.

5

*DeVasher played Lambert a tape of phone calls from
Mitch's hotel room in Memphis to Abby in Massachusetts.*

'Which FBI agent is involved?'

'Tarrance. He seems to be in charge.'

'How often has he talked to Kozinski?'

'There's no way to know. We know of four meetings in the last month, but I suspect more. They're being real careful.'

'How much has he given them?'

'Not much, I hope. They're still trying to persuade him. He's frightened. Hodge hasn't talked to the FBI yet, I don't think. He'll do whatever Kozinski does.'

'What have you told Lazarov?'

'Everything. That's my job. They want you in Chicago the day after tomorrow. They want answers, and plans.'

'What plans?'

'Plans to get rid of Kozinski, Hodge and Tarrance, if it becomes necessary.'

'Tarrance! Are you crazy? We can't get rid of an FBI agent!'

'Lazarov is stupid, Ollie, you know that. And that's what he wants from you. Of course, if he does kill Tarrance, the FBI will be all over the place, and all of you lawyers will suddenly have to leave the country.'

'Try to argue with him, will you? And watch McDeere for another month.'

'OK, Ollie. Don't worry.'

Chapter 4   Sad News

When the McDeeres moved down to Memphis they stayed with the Quins. The two couples became good friends. It didn't take Mitch and Abby long to find a house to buy, on a street called East Meadowbrook. After they moved in they were completely happy. The new house was everything they had dreamed about: large, comfortable and in a good neighbourhood. Abby went mad buying furniture, while Mitch drove the new black BMW all around town, getting to know the area.

The Thursday before Mitch was due to start work they drove over to the Quins' house for dinner.

'Now that you've spent next year's income on furniture,' Mitch said on the way there, 'what next?'

'Oh, I don't know,' Abby said. 'How about babies?'

'Hey, slow down. Let me get settled first!'

Abby laughed and sat back in her seat. Mitch admired her legs.

'When did I last tell you you were beautiful?' he asked.

'About two hours ago.'

'Two whole hours! How thoughtless of me!'

'Right. Don't let it happen again.'

They parked behind the Quins' two Mercedes. Kay met them at the front door. Her eyes were red from crying.

'Oh, Kay, what's the matter?' Abby asked.

'There's . . . there's been a tragedy,' she said.

'Who is it?' Mitch asked.

Kay wiped her eyes and breathed deeply. 'Two members of the firm, Marty Kozinski and Joe Hodge, were killed today. We were very close to them.'

Mitch remembered them from his visit to the firm. 'What happened?' he asked.

'No one's sure,' Kay said. 'They were on Grand Cayman, diving. There was some kind of explosion on the boat and we think they drowned. A boatman was also killed. There was a meeting in the firm a few hours ago and they were all told about it. Lamar could hardly drive home.'

'Where is he?' Mitch asked.

'By the swimming-pool. He's waiting for you.'

Lamar was just sitting there, deep in shock. Mitch sat down next to him and waited. Lamar shook his head and tried to speak, but no words came. His eyes were red and he looked hurt.

Finally, Mitch said, 'Lamar, I'm so sorry. I wish I could say something.'

'There's nothing to say. Marty Kozinski was one of my best friends. He was going to be the next partner. He was a great lawyer, one we all admired. Our . . . our children always played together.'

Mitch and Abby drove home in silence. Four days later, instead of starting behind his desk at the office, Mitch and his lovely wife joined the remaining thirty-nine members of the firm, and their lovely wives, and said goodbye to Marty Kozinski and Joe Hodge. Oliver Lambert gave such a beautiful speech that even Mitchell McDeere, who had buried a father and a brother, was moved close to tears. Abby's eyes watered at the sight of the widows and children.

Chapter 5   Long Hours

Mitch learned fast. He was appointed to work with one of the partners, Avery Tolleson, and helped him with several of his clients. He learned to respect Avery's talent for hard work. Avery taught Mitch all about billing clients for his time. As an associate he could bill $100 an hour. His future progress at the firm, he was warned, depended on how much income he made for the firm. He learned that it was acceptable to bill clients more than he actually worked. 'If you think about a client while you're driving over to the office in the morning,' Avery told him, 'add on another hour.' He could bill clients for twelve hours a day, even if he never worked twelve hours a day. Mitch also learned that Avery liked to bend the firm's rules. His marriage was breaking up and his eyes followed every good-looking woman he saw on the streets. He also drank at lunch-times.

From Avery and the other partners Mitch learned the way things were done at Bendini, Lambert & Locke. He learned that secrecy was valued highly; he learned to talk to no one outside the firm, not even Abby.

Mitch was determined to become a partner in less time than anyone else ever had before. He was determined to earn the firm more money than any associate ever had before. He had heard the stories about how many hours people worked; even sixteen hours a day was not unknown in the firm.

It was said that Nathan Locke started work at six a.m. every day. On his first full day Mitch arrived at the office at 5.30. No one else was there.

He climbed the stairs to his office on the second floor, made himself a cup of coffee and began to work. After a while he got up from his desk and went over to the window. It was still dark outside. He didn't notice the figure suddenly appear at his door.

'Good morning.'

Mitch turned round from the window. 'You frightened me,' he said.

'I'm sorry. I'm Nathan Locke. I don't believe we've met.'

'I'm Mitch McDeere, the new man.' They shook hands.

'Yes, I know.'

Mitch could not stop himself staring at the man's eyes. Nathan Locke's eyes were cold and knowing. They were the most evil eyes he had ever seen.

'I see you're an early riser,' Locke was saying.

'Yes, sir.'

'Well, it's good to have you in the firm.'

◆

After a few days DeVasher, Lambert and Locke had a meeting.

10

They were sure Mitch could not keep going: nobody could work a hundred hours a week for more than a few months.

'How's his wife taking it?' Lambert asked.

'This will change, but at the moment I can only hear his side of the conversations,' DeVasher said. 'She's not delighted. She's practising her cooking for the first time and he's getting sandwiches from the shops, because he's never home in time for dinner.'

'What do you mean, "This will change"?' asked Locke.

'I mean Chicago is still worried, you know? We don't think Kozinski and Hodge told the FBI anything important, but Lazarov wants to be safe. He wants the homes of all associates bugged.'

'Don't you think that's going a bit too far?' asked Lambert.

'Chicago doesn't think so.'

'All of them, even McDeere?'

'Yes. I think Tarrance will try again. Oh, and before I forget, we've found McDeere's brother Ray – or rather, McDeere led us to him. He's in Brushy Mountain Prison, near Nashville. He accidentally killed someone in a bar fight and the court gave him fifteen years. He's done four of them. McDeere went to visit him last Sunday. I wonder if we could use this as a lever against McDeere, if we ever need to.'

Chapter 6   A Tiny Microphone

Mitch didn't slow down: he became a machine. He had never needed as much sleep as other people and now this was to his advantage. However much work Avery Tolleson threw at him, he managed to get through it. Sometimes he worked all through the night, and found an unsmiling Abby waiting for him when he came home at dawn for a quick shower before returning to the office.

Oliver Lambert invited the McDeeres, the Quins and two other associates and their wives to dinner one Saturday at Justine's, his favourite restaurant.

Not long after Mitch and Abby entered the restaurant, two men with the correct key entered the shiny black BMW in the car park of Justine's. They drove away from the restaurant to the new home of Mr and Mrs McDeere. They parked the BMW in its usual place. The driver got another key out of his pocket and the two men entered the house.

They worked quickly and quietly. A tiny microphone, no bigger than a fingernail, was stuck into the mouthpiece of each phone in the house. The signals from these microphones would go to a receiver in the space under the roof of the house.

Then the men turned their attention to each room. A small hole was made in the corner of every room, high up where no one would notice it. A tiny microphone was placed inside each hole. A wire, no thicker than a human hair and completely invisible, ran from each microphone to the receiver. The receiver looked exactly like an old, broken radio, and it joined other old objects that were already there in a corner under the roof. It would not be noticed for months, maybe years. And if it was noticed, it would simply be thrown away as rubbish. The receiver, of course, would also send signals from the house back to the fifth floor at Bendini, Lambert & Locke.

Just as the fish was served at Justine's, the BMW parked quietly next to the restaurant. The driver locked the car door. It was the Mahans next. At least they lived closer to the restaurant than the McDeeres, and had a smaller house, so the work would be easier.

◆

On the fifth floor of the Bendini Building, DeVasher stared at rows of lights and waited for some signal from 1231 East

Meadowbrook. The dinner party had finished thirty minutes earlier and it was time to listen. A tiny yellow light shone weakly and he put a pair of headphones on. He pushed a button to record. He waited. A green light marked 'McD-6' began to shine. It was the bedroom. The voices started to come in loud and clear.

'I don't like Jill Mahan,' the female voice, Mrs McDeere, was saying. 'Her husband's OK, but she's really unpleasant.'

'Are you drunk?' asked Mr McDeere.

'Almost. I'm ready for sex.'

DeVasher bent his head closer towards his surveillance equipment, to listen better.

'Take your clothes off,' Mrs McDeere demanded.

'We haven't done this for a while,' said Mr McDeere.

'And whose fault is that?' she asked.

'I haven't forgotten how. You're beautiful.'

'Get in the bed,' she said.

DeVasher closed his eyes and watched them.

Chapter 7   Tarrance

On the first Monday in August a general meeting was called in the main library on the first floor. Every member was there. The mood was quiet and sad. Beth Kozinski and Laura Hodge were politely brought in by Oliver Lambert. They were seated at the front of the room. In front of them, on the wall, were pictures of their husbands.

Oliver Lambert stood with his back to the wall and gave a speech. He almost whispered at first, but the power of his voice made every sound clear throughout the room. He looked at the two widows and told of the deep sadness the firm felt, and how they would always be taken care of as long as there was a firm. He talked of Marty and Joe, of their first few years with the firm, of their importance to the firm. He spoke of their love for their families.

The widows held hands and cried softly. Kozinski's and Hodge's closest friends, like Lamar Quin and Doug Turney, were wiping their eyes.

After the speech Mitch went over to look at the pictures. There were three other pictures on the wall as well. One was of a woman; underneath the picture were the words 'Alice Knauss, 1948–1977'. He had heard about her: the only woman ever to become a member of the firm, she was killed in a car crash just three years after joining. The other two pictures were of Robert Lamm and John Mickel. He asked Avery about them. Lamm was out hunting in Arkansas one day in 1970 and didn't return. He was found eventually with a bullet in his head. Everyone supposed it was a hunting accident. Mickel shot himself in 1984. Five dead lawyers in fifteen years. It was a dangerous place to work.

♦

Mitch was always the first to arrive at the office and often the last to leave as well. The partners were delighted with his progress and rewarded him with extra money. Abby got a job as a teacher at a local school, so that she wasn't just sitting around the house, bored. Mitch's ability to work long hours was already a legend, but she didn't want to be married to a legend; she wanted a flesh-and-blood person next to her.

Recently Mitch had started having his lunch sometimes in a small café about half a mile from the Bendini Building. It was a dark hole in the wall with few customers and bad food. He liked it because no one else from the firm went there, so he could sit quietly and read legal documents while he ate. He could always bill the client for his time.

One day while he was there a stranger approached his table

The widows held hands and cried softly.

and stood next to it. Mitch put down his document. 'Can I help you?' he asked.

The stranger said, 'You're McDeere, aren't you?'

Mitch studied him. Judging by his accent, he was from New York. He was about forty, with short hair, and was wearing a cheap suit.

'Yeah,' he said. 'Who are you?'

In reply the man pulled a badge out of his pocket. 'Wayne Tarrance, FBI.' He waited for a reaction.

'Sit down,' Mitch said.

'Thanks.' After he sat down, Tarrance said, 'I heard you were the new man at Bendini, Lambert & Locke.'

'Why would that interest the FBI?'

'We watch that firm quite closely.'

'Why?'

'I can't tell you at the moment. We have our reasons, but I didn't come here to talk about them. I came here to meet you, and to warn you about the firm.'

'I'm listening,' Mitch said.

'Three things. First, don't trust anyone. Second, every word you say, at home or in the office, is probably being recorded.'

Mitch watched and listened carefully; Tarrance was enjoying this. 'And the third thing?' he asked.

'Money doesn't grow on trees.'

'What do you mean by that?'

'I can't say more at the moment. I think you and I will become very close. I want you to trust me, and I know I'll have to earn your trust. So I don't want to move too fast. We can't meet at your office or at my office, and we can't talk on the phone. So from time to time I'll come and find you. For now, just remember those three things, and be careful. Here's my home phone number. You won't want to call me yet, but you'll need it sometime. But call me only from a pay phone. If I'm not in, leave a message on the machine.'

Mitch put it in his shirt pocket.

'There's one other thing,' Tarrance said as he stood up. 'You had better know that Hodge's and Kozinski's deaths weren't accidental.' He looked down at Mitch with both hands in his pockets, smiled, and left before Mitch could ask any more questions.

♦

The next day Mitch had an opportunity to go and see Lamar. He walked into his office and closed the door. 'We need to talk,' he said. If he believed Tarrance the office was bugged and the conversation would be recorded. He was not sure whom to believe.

'You sound serious,' Lamar said.

'Did you ever hear of someone called Wayne Tarrance?'

'No.'

'FBI.'

Lamar closed his eyes. 'FBI,' he whispered.

'That's right. He had a badge and everything.'

'Where did you meet him?'

'He found me in Lansky's Café on Union Street. He knew who I was.'

'Have you told Avery?'

'No. No one except you. I'm not sure what to do.'

Lamar picked up the phone and spoke to Avery Tolleson. Within a few minutes Mitch and Lamar were up in Lambert's office. Avery, Lambert, Royce McKnight, Harold O'Kane and Nathan Locke were there, sitting around a conference table.

'Have a seat,' said Locke with a false smile.

'What's that?' Mitch pointed to a tape recorder in the centre of the table.

'We don't want to miss anything,' Locke said.

'OK,' Mitch said. He repeated his conversation with Tarrance.

Locke stared at Mitch with his dark eyes while he was speaking, and as soon as he had finished he asked, 'Have you ever seen this man before?'

'Never.'

'Whom did you tell?'

'Only Lamar.'

'Your wife?'

'No.'

'Did he leave you a phone number to call?'

'No.'

The tape recorder was switched off. Locke walked to the window. 'Mitch,' he said, 'we've had trouble with the FBI and the tax people for several years now. Some of our clients like us to take risks for them. We do things for them which are not quite illegal, but which are close to the edge. And like any firm of tax lawyers with clients as rich as ours, the FBI occasionally has to investigate some of our clients. Naturally, they investigate us at the same time. Tarrance is new down here, and he's trying to score a big win. He's dangerous. You are not to speak to him again.'

'How many of our clients have the courts found guilty?' Mitch asked.

'Not a single one.'

'What about Marty and Joe? What *did* happen?'

'That's a good question. We don't know. It's true that it was possibly not an accident. The boatman who was with them seems to have been a drug smuggler, according to the police there.'

'I don't think we'll ever know,' McKnight added. 'We're trying to protect their families, so we're calling it an accident.'

'Don't mention any of this to anyone,' Locke said. 'Not even your wife. If Tarrance contacts you again, let us know immediately. Understand?'

'Yes, sir.' Mitch nodded.

The grandfatherly warmth returned to Oliver Lambert's face. He smiled and said, 'Mitch, we know this is frightening, but we're used to it. We can look after it. Leave it to us, and don't worry. And stay away from Tarrance.'

'Further contact with Tarrance will put your future in the firm at risk,' Locke said.

'I understand,' Mitch said.

'That's all, Mitch,' Lambert said. 'You and Lamar can go back to work now.'

As soon as they were out of the room Lambert called DeVasher on the phone. Within two minutes Lambert and Locke were sitting in DeVasher's office.

'Did you listen?' Locke asked.

'Yeah, of course. We heard every word the boy said. You handled it very well. I think he's frightened and will run from Tarrance. But I've got to tell Lazarov: he's the boss. I hope I can still persuade him not to kill Tarrance.'

'God, yes,' Lambert said. 'But why did they choose McDeere, do you think?'

'Because he's young and because he's a good person – the kind of person who wouldn't like what's going on here. I suggest you keep McDeere so busy he doesn't have time to think. And it would be a good idea for Quin to get closer to him, too, so that if McDeere does want to tell anyone anything he'll naturally turn to Quin.'

'Did he tell his wife last night?' asked Locke.

'We're checking the tapes now,' DeVasher said. 'It'll take about an hour. We've got so many bugs in this city, it takes six computers to find anything. I'll let you know if I find anything. But he and his wife don't talk that much any more. McDeere had better visit the Caymans, though. Can you arrange it?'

'Of course,' said Lambert. 'But why?'

'I'll tell you later.'

Chapter 8   Four People, Three of them Dead

That Sunday, Mitch went to visit his brother Ray in prison again. There was some information he wanted. They chatted for a while and then Mitch said, 'You once told me in a letter that you knew a prisoner who used to be a cop in Memphis and now works there as a private investigator. I can't remember his name.'

'Eddie Lomax. Yeah. Cops are hated in here. I helped him out once in a fight; they were killing him. We became friends. He still writes to me. He's been out about three years now.'

'Thanks.'

'Why do you need him?'

'A lawyer friend's wife is cheating on him. Is Lomax good?'

'Yeah, I think so. He's made some money, anyway. You'll find him in the phone book.'

A guard walked by and reminded them that it was nearly time for visitors to leave.

'Is there anything I can send you?' asked Mitch. 'Any language tapes?' Ray had learned several languages while he was in prison.

'Yeah, something on Greek, please. And a picture of Abby and of your house. You're the first McDeere in a hundred years to own a house.'

'OK. I'll see you next month.'

♦

Lomax's secretary, Tammy, was blonde, about forty years old but still sexy. She wore short skirts and a low-cut blouse. She kept crossing and uncrossing her legs while Mitch was waiting for Lomax to get off the phone.

When Mitch eventually got into the office Lomax stood up behind his desk and held out his hand. 'So you're Mitchell McDeere. It's good to meet you.'

'My pleasure,' Mitch said. 'I saw Ray on Sunday.'

'I feel like I've known you for years. He talked about you all the time. You look just like him too. Now, what can I do for you? Have you got trouble with your wife?'

'No, nothing like that. I need some information about four people. Three of them are dead.' Mitch told him about the three dead lawyers from Bendini, Lambert & Locke. 'I want to know if there's anything odd about their deaths,' he said.

'Sounds interesting. What about the fourth person?'

'He's called Wayne Tarrance. He's an FBI agent here in Memphis.'

'FBI! That'll cost you more.'

'OK. This must all be absolutely secret, Eddie. I'm trusting you. And don't call me at home or at the office. I suspect I'm being watched very closely.'

'By whom?'

'I wish I knew.'

Chapter 9   Grand Cayman

A week later Avery Tolleson and Mitch left for the Cayman Islands to do some tax work for a client. It was the first time in his life that Mitch had left the country.

They landed on Grand Cayman, a jewel of land surrounded by clear blue sea. Hardly anyone lived on the other two islands, Little Cayman and Cayman Brac, Avery told him. And on Grand Cayman there were only 18,000 people, but 12,000 businesses had their head offices there on paper, and there were 300 banks.

They settled into the firm's apartments on Seven Mile Beach and Avery suggested they go to Rumheads, an open-air bar on the beach. As night fell, Avery was drinking heavily and a pair of sisters joined them at their table. They were dressed only in bikinis. Soon one of them was sitting on Avery's knees and the other one was trying to persuade Mitch to dance with her.

He pushed her away roughly and went for a walk along the beach. In the darkness, all alone on the beach, with only the stars in the sky and the lights of a few boats far away out on the water, another beautiful woman approached him. She reminded him of Abby. They lay on the sand and talked. She quietly took off her bikini – not that there was much of it – and asked Mitch to look after it while she went for a swim. When she came back, rising out of the water and brushing her long wet hair off her face and body, they made love. 'Who will ever know?' Mitch thought. 'I'm not doing anyone any harm.'

◆

In the morning neither of them felt like doing business. In the taxi to the Royal Bank of Montreal, where they had an appointment, Avery cheerfully explained that he was different from the rest of the partners in the firm, because he liked drinking and women. After they had completed their business at the bank Avery went off to meet the woman he had spent the night with, leaving Mitch to wander around the town. They had another appointment at three in the afternoon.

Mitch went to the library and found a newspaper for 27 June of that year. He sat down beside a window to read it. He looked out of the window and saw a man getting out of a car and crossing the street towards the library. He recognized the car: he had also seen it near the bank in the morning. Mitch got up from the table and pretended to be looking at a business magazine in another part of the room.

The man, who was small and dark, came into the library. In a few minutes he appeared in the room where Mitch was. He walked past Mitch, paused as if to check what he was reading, and left the room. When Mitch returned to the window he was back in the car, smoking a cigarette.

Mitch read the newspaper story about the explosion on the boat which had killed two American lawyers and their diving guide. He left the library and, without looking back, walked quickly along narrow, crowded streets, and in and out of shops, until he was sure no one could be following him. Then he caught a taxi to Abanks Diving School. The newspaper had said that the guide who was killed was Philip Abanks, the son of Barry Abanks, who owned the diving school.

Abanks agreed to speak to Mitch. He was certain Philip had nothing to do with drugs. The accident had surprised him because the boat was found a long way from where it was supposed to be, but Philip hadn't used the radio to tell the school about their new position, as an experienced boatman like himself would. He also hadn't radioed about any engine trouble. The boat's engine exploded, but the three bodies were found unharmed, in full diving clothes; they had just drowned, although all three were experienced divers.

♦

A few days later, in Memphis, DeVasher studied the photographs on the desk in front of him. They were of a very high quality. The long-distance night-sight camera had worked well. And the girl was excellent. He would use her again. 'Mitchell McDeere,' he said to himself with a smile, 'now you are ours. Now you'll do anything for us.'

Chapter 10 Dangerous Waters

Two weeks before Christmas, Mitch and Eddie Lomax met on a bridge in a park in the freezing rain. They had both made sure that they were not followed. Lomax's news was very interesting. All three of the dead lawyers had died in mysterious circumstances. The lorry which killed Alice Knauss had been stolen in St Louis three days earlier. The driver drove straight into her car and then ran away. He was never found. The hunter, Robert Lamm, was almost certainly murdered. It didn't look like a hunting accident, because his body was found in a part of the forest where there were few animals and the hunters didn't usually go. There were two strange things about Mickel's death: first, the letter to his wife was typed, not handwritten; second, he had never bought a gun in his life, and yet the gun that killed him was an old gun, which the police thought criminals had used in the past. Where did a respectable lawyer get such a gun?

'Your firm has lost five lawyers in fifteen years,' Lomax ended. 'And you're acting as if you're going to be the next. I'd say you've got problems.'

'What about Tarrance?'

'I don't have very much. He's one of their best men; he came down here from New York about two years ago.'

'Thanks.'

'I'll do anything I can to help Ray McDeere's little brother. It seems to me that you're swimming in dangerous waters.'

Mitch nodded slightly, but said nothing.

♦

Mitch sat in the corner of Paulette's, a French restaurant in the middle of Memphis. At seven o'clock Abby rushed in from the cold and joined him at his table.

'What's the special event?' she asked. Mitch had said hardly

24

anything on the phone when he invited her to meet him here. He was very careful about what he said on the phone these days.

'Do I need a reason to have dinner with my wife?'

'Yes. It's seven o'clock on a Monday night and you're not at the office. That's very unusual.'

A waiter came to their table and they ordered two white wines. As the waiter went away Mitch noticed the face of a man at another table that looked familiar. Before Mitch could think about it the man hid his face behind a menu.

'What's the matter, Mitch?'

He put his hand on hers and said, 'Abby, we've got to talk.'

'What about?' she asked, worried.

'About something very serious,' he said quietly. 'But we can't talk here. There's a back door near the washrooms. I want you to go to the washroom and then leave by the back door. I'll meet you there. I'll bring your coat. Trust me, please.'

Abby left. Mitch waited until the man with the menu was busy talking to a waiter and then he followed her. Outside they walked to a bar and sat down in a dark corner inside.

'What's this all about?' demanded Abby, when they had their drinks.

'I met an FBI agent today, a man called Tarrance. It's the second time he's spoken to me.'

'FBI?'

'Yes. With badges and everything.' He told her about the first meeting with Tarrance and what the partners had said about it.

'What do the FBI want?'

'I don't know, Abby. I'm just eating lunch when someone comes up and tells me that my phones are bugged, my home is bugged, and someone at Bendini, Lambert & Locke knows everything I do. I don't know what they want, Abby, but they've chosen me for some reason.'

'Did you tell anyone at the office?'

'No, I haven't told anyone except you. And I don't intend to tell anyone either.'

Abby drank from her glass of wine. 'Our phones are bugged?'

'According to the FBI. But how do they know?'

'They're not stupid, Mitch. If the FBI told me my phones were bugged I'd believe them.'

'I don't know who to believe. Locke and Lambert were very believable when they explained how the firm fights with the tax people and the FBI. But if the firm did have a rich client whom the FBI was investigating, why would they choose me, the new man in the firm, to talk to? What do I know? I've seen no signs of any criminal acts. All the files I work on are clean.'

'But someone is bugging you.'

'Even the car, Tarrance said.'

'Mitch, this is amazing. Why would a law firm do that?'

'I've no idea. I feel much better now that I've told you. From now on I'll tell you everything. I didn't tell you sooner because I kept hoping it would all go away. And there's more to tell you.' He told her about Eddie Lomax and the five dead lawyers, and how he suspected that none of their deaths was quite what it seemed to be.

'I feel weak.'

'Abby, we have to be careful. We must continue to live as if we suspect nothing.'

'This is unreal, Mitch. I can't believe I'm sitting here listening to you saying all this. Do you expect me to live in a house where everything's bugged?'

'Do you have a better idea?'

'Yeah. Let's hire this Eddie Lomax to inspect our house.'

'This is unreal, Mitch. Do you expect me to live
in a house where everything's bugged?'

'I've thought of that. But what if he finds something? Think about it. What if we know for sure that the house is bugged? What then? What if he breaks one of the bugs? Then whoever put them there will know that we know, and that could be dangerous.'

'You're right. Anyway, you're hardly home for me to talk to. They'll only hear me talking to myself a lot these days.'

Chapter 11   A Professional Job

A day or two after Christmas, Eddie Lomax was called out on an urgent job. A man calling himself Al Kilbury said that his wife was about to meet a man in a hotel in south Memphis and that he needed Lomax to take photographs. He tempted him with an offer of generous payment. They drove to the hotel together and waited in the car park. Another man silently opened the back door of the car and put three bullets into the back of Lomax's head. It was a professional job. The killer and the man calling himself Al Kilbury left together.

◆

Mitch found the bar near the airport where Tammy had asked him to meet her. He looked again at the letter she had pinned to the back door of his house: 'Dear Mr McDeere, Please meet me at Ernie's Bar on Winchester Avenue late tonight. It's about Eddie Lomax. Very important. Tammy Hemphill, his secretary.'

Tammy arrived soon after he had ordered a beer. 'Thanks for coming,' she said.

'What's the matter?'

She looked round. 'We need to talk, but not here.'

'Where do you suggest?'

'Why don't we drive around? We'll take my car.'

In the car she took a long time to say what she wanted to say. Eventually it started to come out.

'You heard about Eddie?' she asked.

'Yes.'

'When did you last meet him?'

'A couple of weeks before Christmas.'

'I thought so. He didn't keep any file about the work he was doing for you.' There was a pause. 'Eddie and I were . . . we were lovers. My marriage isn't so great, and my husband has other women friends. Anyway, Eddie told me a little about you and he said that lawyers from your firm kept dying.'

So much for secrecy, Mitch thought.

'Anyway, just before Christmas he told me he thought he was being followed and that he thought it was connected to the work he was doing for you. Eddie was good at his job. It wouldn't be easy to follow him. They were professionals, whoever they were − as professional as the killer. I'm frightened, Mitch. Can I call you Mitch?'

'Of course.'

'I haven't been back to the office since his death. They probably think I know whatever it is that he knew.'

'You're right not to take any chances,' Mitch said.

'We can disappear for a while, my husband and I. He works as a singer in nightclubs and he can always get work somewhere else.'

'That sounds like a good idea. Where will you go?'

'Here and there,' she said. 'They've killed all those lawyers, and they've killed Eddie, and next they want you and me.'

'We need to keep in touch, Tammy,' Mitch said, 'but you can't talk to me on the phone and we shouldn't meet. Write to me once a week from wherever you are. What's your mother's name?'

'Doris.'

'Fine. Sign your letters Doris.'

'Do they read your mail, too?'

'Probably, Doris, probably.'

Chapter 12   Denton Voyles

Mitch flew into Washington on the firm's private jet. DeVasher didn't want him to go. Chicago had given orders that McDeere was not to leave Memphis on firm business except with at least two partners. But the firm had arranged months ago for Mitch to go to this conference on taxes in Washington. DeVasher couldn't argue against it, because as far as he knew Tarrance had only met Mitch that one time, and Mitch had immediately reported it. So Mitch seemed to be a loyal member of the firm.

His first morning at the conference, surrounded by strangers, a man whispered, 'Harbison, FBI,' and passed him a note. The note read:

Dear Mr McDeere

I would like to speak to you for a few minutes during lunch. Please follow Grant Harbison's instructions. Thank you for your co-operation.

F. Denton Voyles

Voyles was the almost legendary boss of the FBI. Harbison arranged a meeting in the men's room. He went first and Mitch followed after twenty minutes.

'What does Voyles want?' he asked.

'Something important. It's not my job to tell you,' said Harbison. 'When the conference breaks for lunch you'll find a taxi, number 8667, outside the hotel. It will take you to the meeting. Be careful: two of the boys from Memphis followed you here. They're in the bedroom next to you in the hotel.'

♦

Mitch followed his instructions. The driver of the taxi spoke to others constantly on his radio. When he was certain that no one was following them he stopped acting like a tour guide and took Mitch directly to his meeting with Voyles in another hotel. Tarrance was waiting in the hotel room.

After a few minutes Voyles walked in with another agent. Voyles offered his hand and Mitch stood up to shake it.

'Thank you for coming,' Voyles said. 'This is very important to us.'

Mitch breathed deeply. 'Sir, do you have any idea how confused and frightened I am? I really need an explanation. What's happening?'

'Mitch, what I'm about to tell you will certainly shock you. You won't want to believe it. But it's all true, and with your help we can save your life.'

Mitch waited.

'No lawyer has ever left your firm alive,' Voyles went on. 'Three have tried, and they were killed. Two others were about to leave, and they died last summer. When a lawyer joins Bendini, Lambert & Locke, he never leaves, unless he retires and keeps his mouth shut. And by the time they retire they are part of it all and cannot talk. The firm has a major surveillance operation on the fifth floor. Your house, car and phones are bugged. Your desk and office are bugged. Almost every word you speak is heard and recorded on the fifth floor. They follow you, and sometimes your wife. You see, Mitch, the firm is not what it seems. It is not owned by the partners. It is part of a very large and very illegal business. The firm of Bendini, Lambert & Locke is owned by the Morolto crime family in Chicago. The Mafia.'

'I don't believe it,' Mitch said, frozen with fear. His voice was weak.

Voyles smiled. 'Yes, you do, Mitch. You've suspected something for some time. That's why you talked to Abanks in the Caymans. That's why you hired that investigator and got him killed by those boys on the fifth floor. You know the firm is rotten, Mitch.'

Mitch rested his head in his hands and stared at the floor.

'As far as we can see,' Voyles said, 'about a quarter of the firm's clients and businesses are legal. There are some very good lawyers in the firm, doing tax work for rich clients. It's a very good cover. Most of the files you've worked on so far are OK. That's how they operate. They bring in a new man, throw money at him, buy the car and house, take him to the Caymans and put him to work on their legal clients. Then after five or six years, when the money is really good, when you and your family have become completely used to this rich way of living, they tell the truth. By then you can't get out even if you want to. They'll kill your wife, or one of your children; they don't care. So you stay. You can't leave. If you stay, you make a million dollars and retire young with your family safe. If you try to leave, your picture will hang in the first-floor library.'

'You mean that *every* partner...?' Mitch couldn't finish.

'Yes, they all know and they all do what they're told. We suspect that most of the associates know as well. We don't think the wives do. We really want these people. We could destroy the Morolto family. We could arrest hundreds of them.'

'How do they help the Moroltos?' Mitch asked.

'To be honest,' Voyles said, 'we don't know everything. We've only been watching them for about seven years, and very little information gets out. But here's an example. A partner takes several million dollars in "dirty" money to the Caymans on the firm's private jet.'

Mitch thought of all the journeys the partners kept making to the Caymans. Voyles continued his story.

'Then the same partner, or one of the others, forms a legal company back in the States, to buy some land perhaps. The money is wired through from the Caymans to . . . what's the name of that bank in St Louis with whom the firm does a lot of business?'

'Commercial Guaranty?'

'That's the one. The Mafia own it. So the money arrives back in the States and is used legally. Suddenly, "dirty" money is "clean". That's why Bendini was sent down there in 1944. Locke grew up working for the Moroltos. He's a criminal first and a lawyer second. Lambert is the perfect cover for the firm. He looks and sounds like everyone's idea of a lawyer. But the next time you see him in the office, Mitch, remember that he's a killer.'

'What about the secretaries and support staff?'

'Good question. We think some of them are part of it too. But some of them don't know anything. That's how they operate as two firms at once: a lot of the people there really are doing legal business. But Hodge told Tarrance that there's a group of support staff who work only for the main partners of the firm. They probably do all their legal work, so that the partners are free to do the Moroltos' dirty business.'

'If you know so much, why don't you just go in there and arrest them all?' asked Mitch.

'We need evidence,' Voyles said. 'That's where you come in. We want you to photocopy files, bank records, all those documents which we can't reach from the outside but you can. We need the names of all the staff; we need to know who works on which files; we need all the information you can give us, about every part of Bendini, Lambert & Locke. And then eventually we'll want you to appear in court and be a witness – our most important witness. You must decide whether or not you'll co-operate, Mitch. Tell us soon. If you decide not to help us, we'll find someone else who will, sooner or later, and we'll put you in prison along with the rest of them. If you choose to help us, we can negotiate a price. And then we'll look after you, send you and your wife anywhere in the world you want to go.'

'But the Mafia never forgets,' Mitch said. 'I've heard stories of witnesses hidden by the FBI whose car suddenly explodes. You people are capable of mistakes; one day, in ten years' time, one of you will talk to the wrong person. If I help you I'll always live in fear. I'll never be able to practise law again; Abby and I will have to change our faces and become Mr and Mrs Ordinary in Nowheretown.'

'It's true, Mitch,' Voyles said. 'They never forget. But I promise you, we will look after you and your wife. We have about two thousand witnesses living all over the country under new names, with new homes and new jobs. Now you had better get back to your hotel. Tarrance will make contact with you soon.'

Chapter 13   Shopping for Shoes

Abby met him at the airport and in the bar he told her everything that had happened. She was frightened and close to tears, but neither of them could see any way out. They couldn't just run away and they couldn't do nothing. Even while they were talking Mitch saw a tall, fair-haired man with a moustache at the bar whom he remembered from the hotel in Washington. They were following him all the time.

Tarrance didn't wait long. A week after Mitch returned to Memphis, about the same time that 'Doris' got in contact, Tarrance met him as he was walking back from a meeting and suggested they turn into a shoe shop together, to get off the street. He started to say that it was time for Mitch to decide what to do, but he suddenly stopped.

*Tarrance started to say that it was time for Mitch to
decide what to do, but he suddenly stopped.*

'What is it?' Mitch demanded.

'I just saw someone walk by the shop and look in at us. Listen carefully, Mitch. We'll walk out together, and as soon as we're outside, you push me away and shout at me. Then run in the direction of the office.'

Mitch did exactly as Tarrance suggested. As soon as he got back to the Bendini Building he went to Avery Tolleson's office and reported that the same FBI agent had contacted him again. By the time they got to Locke's office, Lambert and McKnight were there as well.

He pretended to be frightened and upset, and demanded to know why the FBI had now contacted him twice. Lambert told him the same story as before. Mitch hardly heard him; he watched his lips moving and thought of Kozinski and Hodge and their families. Then Locke asked him what had happened today.

'Tarrance pushed me into the shoe shop. I tried to run away, but Tarrance followed me and grabbed me. I pushed him away and ran back here. That's all that happened. What shall I do?'

'Nothing, Mitch,' said Lambert. 'Just stay away from this Tarrance. If he even looks at you, report it to us immediately.'

'That's what he did,' said Avery.

Mitch tried to look as pitiful as possible.

'You can go, Mitch,' Lambert said.

♦

'He's lying. I'm sure he's lying,' DeVasher said. They were all in DeVasher's office.

'What did your man see?' asked Locke.

'Something slightly different, but at the same time very different, you know? He says McDeere and Tarrance walked together into the shoe shop. He didn't see Tarrance grab

McDeere. They're in the shop for a couple of minutes. Our man walks by and looks inside. Next minute they're fighting on the street. Something isn't right, I tell you.'

The partners thought for a while. Finally, Oliver Lambert said, 'Look, DeVasher, it's possible that McDeere is telling the truth and that your man got the wrong signals. You don't know of any contact since last August.'

'No, but we can't watch anybody absolutely all the time. We didn't know about those other two until it was almost too late.'

'But because you don't know of any recent contact, you shouldn't doubt what McDeere's saying.'

'I'm not sure,' said DeVasher. 'I think McDeere and I should have a little talk.'

'About what?' Lambert asked nervously.

'Just leave it to me. If you fools were in charge of security we'd all be in prison by now. Lazarov is getting really worried, but he thinks he can get someone in the FBI to talk. Then we'll know whether McDeere is lying.'

♦

Mitch was alone in his office late that night when a short, fat man walked in. 'My name's DeVasher,' he said.

'What can I do for you?' Mitch asked.

'You can listen for a while. I'm in charge of security for the firm . . .'

'Why does the firm need security?' Mitch asked.

'Bendini was crazy about security. Anyway, we believe the FBI are trying to get a man inside the firm to help in their investigations of some of our clients. It's important that you tell us whenever they attempt to make contact with you.'

'Yes, I already know that.'

Suddenly DeVasher was smiling evilly. 'I brought something with me to show you,' he said. 'Something that will keep you honest.' He reached inside his jacket and pulled out an envelope.

Mitch opened it nervously. Inside were four photographs, black and white, very clear. On the beach. The girl.

'Oh, my God! Who took these?' Mitch shouted at him.

'What difference does that make?'

Mitch tore the photographs up and let the pieces fall on to his desk.

'We've got plenty more upstairs,' DeVasher said calmly. 'We don't want to use them, but if we catch you talking to Mr Tarrance or some other FBI agent, we'll send them to your wife. How would you like that, Mitch? The next time you and Tarrance decide to shop for shoes, think about us, Mitch. Because we'll be watching.'

Chapter 14   Two Black Briefcases

'So you want to rent a small office?' the agent said as they rode up in the lift. He was admiring the tight jeans on the blonde.

She smiled and nodded.

The lift stopped and they got out. He showed her the small two-room office. She liked it. They negotiated a price – a good price for even a small office on the ninth floor of the famous Cotton Shipping Building. She signed the forms 'Doris Greenwood'.

By noon the next day the furniture was in place. There was a knock at the door. 'Who is it?' she asked.

'It's your photocopier,' a voice answered.

She unlocked the door and opened it. Two men wheeled in a big machine and she pointed them towards the spare second room.

'It's a big copier for such a small office,' one of them

remarked. 'This is the most modern machine we've got. It does ninety copies a minute.'

She smiled and said it would do fine and signed the documents. After they had gone she locked the door behind them and walked to the window. She looked north, along Front Street. A quarter of a mile away, on the opposite side, the Bendini Building was visible.

♦

On a Tuesday morning Mitch's secretary checked that he had everything for his meeting with Frank Mulholland in fifteen minutes. Mitch, sitting at his desk, pointed at a large black briefcase. He finished signing the letters on the desk in front of him, picked up the briefcase and a thin document case and left the building. He checked that the briefcase was in his right hand and the document case in his left. That was the signal.

On the ninth floor of the Cotton Shipping Building, Tammy moved away from the window, put on her coat and left the office.

Mitch entered the building and went straight to the lifts. Mulholland's office was on the seventh floor. Mitch pushed the button. He was not alone in the lift, but he didn't think they had followed him here. He put the briefcase down on the floor by his foot.

Tammy got into the lift on the fourth floor. She had brought with her exactly the same kind of briefcase that Mitch had. She didn't look at Mitch but stood next to him and put her briefcase down on the floor next to his. On the seventh floor Mitch picked up her briefcase and left the lift; on the ninth floor Tammy picked up his briefcase and went to her office.

The briefcase was full of files from Bendini, Lambert & Locke. Tammy locked the door behind her. There were seven thick files. She laid them on the table next to the copier. She took the papers out of the first file and put them into the copier. She pushed the 'Print' button and watched the machine make two perfect copies of every page.

Mitch's meeting with Mulholland went well. They shook hands at the end and arranged another meeting next week.

The lift stopped on the fifth floor and Tammy walked in. It was empty except for Mitch. When the door closed he said, 'Any problems?'

'No. Two copies are locked away.'

'How long did it take?'

'Thirty minutes.'

The lift stopped on the fourth floor and she picked up the empty briefcase. 'Midday tomorrow?' she asked.

'Yes,' he replied. The door opened and she disappeared on to the fourth floor. He rode alone down to the ground floor and walked, with a briefcase in each hand, looking just as a lawyer should, back to his office.

Chapter 15   Secret Talks

A week later Mitch was having lunch with the partners in their fifth-floor dining-room. Each year every associate member was invited twice. Throughout lunch Mitch knew that he was being watched very closely. They were looking for any signs that he was a less keen member of the firm than he used to be. So he forced himself to smile and to eat the food they offered him. It was impossible for him to forget the pictures of him and the girl in the sand. Had they all seen the pictures? Had they passed them around this table?

Oliver Lambert had never been so charming. He told stories about past members of the firm, congratulated Mitch on the hours he was working and the amount of money he was earning the firm, and said he deserved the holiday he was taking next week.

'You and your wife are off to the Caymans, I hear,' Royce McKnight said. 'You'll love it there.'

'Do you dive?' asked Lambert.

'No, but we plan to do plenty of swimming,' Mitch said.

'If you want to learn to dive,' Lambert went on, 'there's a man called Adrian Bench who has an excellent diving school on the north end of the island. It's worth a visit.'

In other words, stay away from Abanks, Mitch thought. 'Thanks. I'll remember that,' he said.

'But be careful, Mitch,' Lambert said. 'It brings back memories of Marty and Joe.'

The partners looked down sadly at their plates. Mitch felt sick. They had killed Marty and Joe for doing exactly what he was doing. He wanted two million from the FBI. There were a couple of other things he wanted too.

♦

At the same time that Mitch was having lunch with the partners, Tammy Greenwood Hemphill parked her dirty brown Volkswagen behind the shiny Peugeot in the school car park. She left the engine running. She got out of the car, pulled a key from her pocket, opened the back of the Peugeot and took the heavy black briefcase out. Then she drove away in her own car.

At a small window in the teachers' lounge Abby drank coffee and stared through the trees into the car park. She smiled and checked her watch. Twelve-thirty, as planned.

Tammy drove back to her office. No one followed her; no one knew of her existence. There were nine files this time. He had said there would eventually be about forty. She copied them all. On the way back to the school she took all the copied files to the small storage room she had rented in her name.

◆

At three o'clock in the morning Mitch got quietly out of bed and got dressed. Without a word he kissed Abby, who was awake, and left the house. He had a meeting at an all-night café twenty-five miles out of town. At this time of night no one would follow him.

Tarrance and he completed their negotiations. They agreed on two million dollars.

'I want a million now and a million later,' Mitch said. 'I'm already copying all my files. No lawyer is allowed to do that: as soon as I give them to you, it's the end of my career. So when I give them to you I want the first million. We'll discuss the details later.'

'How are you going to get the files to us?' Tarrance asked. 'You can't just walk around with them.'

'That's right,' Mitch said. 'When I hear that the first million has gone where I want it to go, then I'll give you the key to a storage room somewhere in the Memphis area.'

'And the second million?' Tarrance asked.

'When you and I and Voyles decide that I've given you enough documents to make the arrests you want, then I get half. After I appear in court as a witness for the last time, I get the other half.'

'Agreed,' Tarrance said.

'And there's one other thing I want, Tarrance.'

'Yeah?'

'I want my brother Ray out of Brushy Mountain Prison.'

'That's ridiculous, Mitch. We can't do that.'

'You can find a way. If you can't do it by bending the rules, then you can help him escape. But you can do it. The FBI can do anything, remember?'

'I'll see what I can do,' Tarrance said helplessly. 'But Voyles isn't going to like it.'

'Tell him that he doesn't get to see anything – not a single file – unless he promises to get my brother out. Not even a file on one of my clean clients. I don't know why you want those files anyway.'

'Because when we've got them,' Tarrance said, 'we've got you. Actually, you're probably already working with criminal clients without knowing it. It makes it easier for the firm to persuade you later to do whatever they say, because they'll tell you that you've already done enough to go to prison.'

Chapter 16 No Kiss

At eight o'clock on the morning after Mitch and Abby returned from the Caymans, Oliver Lambert and Nathan Locke were allowed through the metal door on the fifth floor. They went to DeVasher's office.

'I talked to Lazarov yesterday in Las Vegas. He's still worried. He wants you to make sure that any associates who don't know about our real business here work only on clean files.'

'OK. What about McDeere?' Lambert asked.

'He had a wonderful week with his wife. They stayed in the other house, of course. You should see her in a string bikini! We took some pictures, just for fun.'

'I didn't come here to look at pictures,' Locke said angrily.

'All right, all right. They spent a whole day with our friend Abanks. We don't know what they talked about. Whenever we got someone close to them, they were only talking about fishing or something. But I don't like it at all.'

'What can they talk about?' said Lambert. 'Of course they'll talk about Hodge and Kozinski, but there's no harm in that. They can't find anything out, can they?'

'No,' DeVasher admitted, 'but I still don't like it. I know

43

McDeere tells lies. I know he lied about that shoe shop. And Chicago is worried, so I'm worried. That's my job. As long as the FBI are around, I'll be worried.'

◆

It was very unusual for wives to appear at the Bendini Building. Abby arrived there unexpectedly. The receptionist phoned up to Mitch's office and his secretary came down to explain that Mitch was in a meeting.

'He's always in a meeting,' Abby replied. 'Get him out of it!'

She waited in Mitch's office. He was on the third floor, in Avery's office, helping him prepare for another visit to the Caymans. Probably taking cash for the Moroltos, Mitch thought. His secretary found him there and told him about Abby.

He walked down to his office, where Abby was walking up and down.

'Mitch, I have to go and see my parents,' she said. 'My father just called me at school. My mother's ill. She's got to have an operation tomorrow.'

'I'm sorry,' Mitch said. He didn't touch her. She wasn't crying.

'I've told the school I'll be away for a while,' she said.

'How long?'

'I don't know. Mitch, we need some time away from each other. I think it will be good for both of us.'

'Let's talk about it.'

'You're always too busy to talk. I've been trying to talk to you for six months, but you can't hear me. I'll be back, I promise. I just don't know when. I love you, Mitch.'

He watched her open the door. There was no kiss.

◆

On the fifth floor an engineer pushed the emergency button for

DeVasher's office. He came immediately and put headphones on. He listened.

'When did this happen?'

'Two minutes ago. In his office, second floor.'

'She's leaving him, isn't she? Hell! She's our best lever. What good are those photographs if she's leaving him anyway?'

♦

Abby started for Kentucky but didn't arrive there. She made sure that she wasn't being followed and then went to Nashville Airport. From there she flew to the Caymans.

♦

Avery finished his business at the Royal Bank of Montreal and, after changing his clothes, made his way to Rumheads Bar. Just after he arrived Tammy nervously entered the crowd and sat at the bar. She was wearing a bikini which hardly covered her body. She was forty, but twenty pairs of hungry eyes followed her to the bar, where she ordered a soft drink and lit a cigarette.

She went over to Avery's table and asked if she could sit down. He couldn't believe his luck; of all the men in the bar she had picked him.

'I'm Avery Tolleson. From Memphis.'

'Nice to meet you. I'm Libby.'

'What brings you here?' Avery asked.

'Just looking for fun,' she said, with a suggestive look in her eyes.

For three hours they dined, drank and danced, each time a little more closely. She got him drunk. At ten o'clock she led him from the bar to the firm's beach house where he was staying. He attacked her at the front door and they kissed long and deeply.

When they were inside she suggested that they should have

She took a small plastic packet from her bag and dropped
some sleeping-powder into his drink.

one more drink. He left the room to go to the washroom. She took a small plastic packet from her bag and dropped some sleeping-powder into his drink. Mitch had told her it was enough to put him to sleep for ten hours. When he returned, she watched closely as he swallowed his drink. He was too drunk to taste a thing. Within minutes he was in a deep sleep.

She pushed him off the chair and pulled him into the bedroom. She laid him on the bed and took his clothes off. She kissed him goodnight.

In his jacket pocket she found two key-rings, with eleven keys on them. Downstairs, in the hall between the kitchen and the sitting-room, she found the mysterious metal door which Mitch had noticed when he stayed in this house with Avery last year. From the arrangement of the upstairs rooms Mitch guessed that there was a small room behind the door.

She opened the door, waited a full ten minutes for any alarm and then turned on the light. Inside the room were twelve cupboards for files, a desk and three large briefcases.

She checked that Avery was still deeply asleep. Then she went back downstairs, grabbed the three briefcases, turned off the lights and left through the front door. It was a short walk across the car park to where the neighbouring hotel started. She was sweating from the weight of the briefcases by the time she reached Room 188 and knocked on the door.

Abby opened the door. 'Any problems?' she asked.

'No.' Tammy put the briefcases on the bed and went to get a Coke.

'Where is he?'

'In bed. I think we've got until six in the morning. There are a hell of a lot of files in that room. We'll be lucky to finish by six.'

Room 188 was a single hotel room. All the furniture had been pushed against the walls to make room for the photocopier Abby had rented.

Tammy began to photocopy the files from the briefcases while Abby went out in her car and had the keys copied by a man she had found earlier. When she came back she continued with the photocopying, while Tammy went back to the beach house. She filled two suitcases with files from the cupboards. By the time she got back to the hotel Abby had finished with the briefcases, and Tammy took them back. Her arms soon ached from carrying the suitcases full of files from one place to the other.

They managed to copy the files from ten of the cupboards before Avery showed any signs of beginning to wake up. She left the files they were copying with Abby, went back to the beach house, locked the metal door and returned the keys. Then she took off her bikini top, got into bed beside him and waited.

♦

Avery finally woke up a few minutes after nine. He felt terrible. He was late for an appointment.

'Hello, big boy,' Tammy said. 'You were wonderful.'

Avery tried to remember something about last night. He failed.

'Was I?' he said.

'Yeah, the best,' she said. He began to believe her.

'Listen,' he said. 'I have to take a shower and then go to work. Shall we meet tonight at the bar?'

'I'll be there, lover,' she said.

He went off to the shower. She slid across the bed to the phone and called Abby.

'He's in the shower.'

'Are you OK?'

'Yeah. He couldn't do it if he had to.'

'Does he suspect anything?'

'I don't think so. He's in pain.'

'How long will you be?'

'About ten or fifteen minutes.'

'OK. Hurry.'

They put their phones down. Under the roof, a recorder switched itself off and was ready for the next phone call.

Chapter 17   Tarry Ross

While Avery was at work the two women finished the last two cupboards of files. They had a mountain of photocopied pieces of paper. By two-thirty in the afternoon it was all in boxes in a storage room in Georgetown. Over the next few days Tammy flew in and out of the Caymans and carried the papers to a one-room apartment in Brentwood, near Nashville. There she started the long job of listing and describing all the contents. Mitch had told her it was urgent.

♦

Tarrance was surprised when Abby came to the meeting instead of Mitch. But she was no less efficient. She gave him the instructions for wiring the first million dollars to a bank in Freeport, in the Bahamas.

'And when do we get the files?' Tarrance asked.

'As soon as we hear the money's in Freeport, we'll send you a key to a storage room somewhere in Memphis. Any questions?'

'Yes. Are you making progress in getting the dirty files?'

She smiled. 'We already have most of what we need. By the time we finish we'll have ten thousand dirty files for you.'

Tarrance was excited. 'Where are they?'

'Not with the clean files, I promise you.'

'But you have them?'

'Yes. Would you like to see a couple?'

'Of course.'

'You can – as soon as Ray is out of prison.'

♦

Tarry Ross was known to the Palumbo family as 'Alfred'. The fewer people who knew his real name, the better; then his employers, the FBI, would never hear about his profitable extra work. The Palumbo family decided to help the Morolto family. Lazarov told them he wanted some information out of the FBI. The Palumbos said they would do it for half a million. Lazarov agreed, and Vinnie Cozzo from the Palumbo family met Ross.

'Make it quick, Cozzo,' Ross said nervously.

'Did you ever hear of the Bendini firm in Memphis?' Cozzo asked.

'No.' The rule was always to say no at first. And always make them wait: that way the price went up. Of course he'd heard of Bendini, Lambert & Locke.

Vinnie went on, 'There's someone down there named Mitchell McDeere, who works for this Bendini firm. We want to know if he's been talking to your people. We think he's selling information to the FBI. We just want to know if we're right, you know? That's all.'

Ross listened with a straight face, though it wasn't easy. He knew everything about McDeere. He knew that McDeere had met Tarrance half a dozen times now. He knew that tomorrow McDeere was suddenly going to get a million dollars.

'I'll see what I can do,' he said. 'How much?'

'Two hundred thousand.'

'In cash?' Ross said in amazement.

'Yeah. You can see we're real serious about this. Can you do it?'

'Yes.'

'When?'

'Give me two weeks.'

Chapter 18   Fitting the Pieces Together

In the weeks before the end of the tax year everyone in the firm was especially busy. With no wife to go home to, Mitch worked later than anyone else. Besides, he had extra work to do. One night, at three in the morning, he unlocked Avery's office on the fourth floor with one of the keys Abby had given him. He remembered a lot of the names of the files on Tammy's list. He unlocked the file cupboards and found what he was looking for.

He carried the papers over to the photocopier near Avery's office. Every file in the firm had a number, and none of the copiers in the building would start until they were programmed with a file number. Mitch programmed the machine with the number of an innocent file which was sitting on his desk downstairs, and copied all 128 pieces of paper. He returned this file to Avery's office and came back with another one. He programmed in a different number. That night he used eighteen file numbers from his own files and three he borrowed from Lamar Quin's files.

A wire led from the copier through a hole in the wall and down the inside of a cupboard, where it joined wires from three other copiers on the fourth floor. This new, larger wire ran down to the third floor, where a computer recorded every copy made within the firm, so that they could bill the proper client. An innocent-looking grey wire ran from this computer up through the fourth floor to the fifth, where another computer recorded the same information, and added the details of which machine was used to make the copies.

♦

DeVasher was trying to fit the pieces together. Something was wrong, but he couldn't work out what it was. He voiced his thoughts to Lambert and Locke.

'His wife leaves, saying her mother's got to have an operation and that she's tired of him. Right? But from the conversations we've recorded, things weren't that bad between them. And why can't we find a hospital that's heard of Maxine Sutherland? We've checked every hospital in Kentucky, Indiana and Tennessee. Doesn't that seem odd to you?'

'Not really,' Lambert said. 'People often use hospitals on the other side of the country if that's where the specialist doctor is. And her parents are rich people. They'd find the best medical help, wherever it was.'

Locke nodded and agreed. 'How much has he talked to her?'

'She calls about once a day. All they talk about is her mother and his work and stuff like that.'

'Hasn't she mentioned the name of the hospital?' asked Locke.

'Not once. Sometimes I think it's a trick to get her out of town, to protect her.'

'I can't believe that,' Lambert said. 'There's no proof of that.'

DeVasher looked angrily at them and walked nervously up and down behind his desk. 'About ten days ago, someone made a lot of unusual copies on the fourth floor. At three o'clock in the morning. At the time, only McDeere and Scott Kimble were in the building. Neither of them has any business on the fourth floor. Twenty-one file numbers were used. Three belong to Lamar Quin's files and the other eighteen all belong to McDeere's files. None belong to Kimble. The copier used was the one nearest to Avery's office, and McDeere works closely with Avery. Who do *you* think made the copies?'

'How many?'

'Just over two thousand.'

'Which files?'

'His own tax clients. At this time of year that seems fine, doesn't it? But five days later his secretary used the same eighteen file numbers to make three hundred copies. It seems to me that three hundred copies is what you'd expect for tax clients at this time of year. But two thousand?'

Locke and Lambert were listening closely now.

'So what was he copying?' DeVasher continued. 'I don't know. But Avery's got cupboards in his office where the real files are kept.'

'He couldn't copy those files,' Lambert said.

'What else was he copying, Ollie? If he and Tarrance are talking, what else would he want from Avery's office?'

'How could he get Avery's keys?' Locke asked.

'That's the question, isn't it?' DeVasher said. 'Avery says he keeps them with him all the time. He also says that, when he was on the Caymans three weeks ago, he slept alone both nights. But he's lying. Listen to this.'

He played them the recorded phone conversation between Tammy and Abby.

'Who are those women?' Locke demanded.

'We don't know. The one in his house must be someone he brought home from a bar. But why is she calling a friend? It's too much to think that these women took his keys and managed to copy them in the middle of the night without his knowing anything about it. And that they are friends of McDeere's.'

'I agree,' said Lambert.

'What about all the secret files in the beach house?' asked Locke.

'I've thought about that, Nat. Let's say she had the keys – though that's unlikely – and let's say she opened the room and found the files. What's she going to do with them in the middle of the night with Avery asleep upstairs?'

'She could read them.'

'I don't think so. There are too many of them.'

'She could be working for the FBI.'

'No, definitely not,' DeVasher said. 'She's no professional. No professional would make a phone call like that. I can only think that she and her friend were after his wallet, and something went wrong.'

Locke and Lambert agreed.

'But we've got to be safe,' DeVasher said. 'I want all the locks changed on the third and fourth floors, and in the beach house. I want everyone on Grand Cayman who can copy keys questioned. And Avery's a risk. I want him to leave for a while. Pretend he's ill or something and has to take time off work.'

◆

On Saturday, Mitch went to visit Ray in prison. By talking in Spanish, and when the guards were nowhere near them, Mitch warned him to be ready to escape in a few days' time.

When he got back to Memphis he parked his BMW in the centre of town.

The fair-haired man with a moustache, whose name was Aaron Rimmer, called DeVasher. 'He's only gone shopping,' he said. 'I'll stay with the car until he comes back for it.'

Mitch walked into a shop and used a pay phone to call for a taxi to meet him at the side entrance in ten minutes. The taxi took him to the apartment at Brentwood. He knocked on the door.

'Who is it?' a nervous female voice asked from inside. He heard the voice and felt weak.

'Barry Abanks,' he said.

Abby opened the door and rushed into his arms.

After an hour on the bed the pain of loneliness was forgotten. They walked through the small apartment holding hands and kissing. Mitch saw for the first time the enormous amounts of paper. He had seen Tammy's notes and lists but not the actual papers. One day soon he would spend hours here, studying the papers and preparing his evidence.

Chapter 19   Avery's Illness

On Monday morning Mitch's secretary told him that Lambert wanted to see him. 'But don't forget that you're due at Mulholland's office in the Cotton Shipping Building soon,' she added.

Up in Lambert's office they talked for a while about Avery's illness. Lambert sounded worried about him.

'I visited him in hospital yesterday,' Mitch said. 'He seemed OK. It's his heart, the doctors said.'

'Anyway,' Lambert said, 'he's going to be away for two months. While he's away, I want you to work with Victor Milligan. But before you start, Avery's got some unfinished business in the Caymans. I want you to go down there tomorrow on the private jet. Tomorrow morning I'll give you a file about the clients to read on the jet. OK?'

'Of course. No problem.'

But he was thinking: something is wrong here.

♦

He met Tammy in her office in the Cotton Shipping Building.

'I want you to call Tarrance,' he said. 'Ask him to investigate Avery Tolleson's illness. I'm not sure it's real.'

'OK.'

'Did you talk to Abanks?'

'Yes.'

'Did he get the money?'

'Yes. It was wired on Friday.'

'Is he ready?'

'He said he was.'

'Good. What about the man who's making us new documents?'

'They call him the Doctor. I'm meeting him this afternoon. He's an old friend of Eddie's. Eddie said he was the best in the country.'

'I hope so. We need new names. Are you OK for money?'

'I've nearly finished the fifty thousand you gave me.'

'How about another fifty thousand?'

'Fine.'

They smiled at each other as he left.

♦

Late that night Ray McDeere walked out of prison. It was as easy as that. A guard came to fetch him. 'I don't know who your friends are,' he said, 'but they must be important.' He took him out to the prison walls. 'The lights are going to go off for a while,' he said. 'You'll find a rope ladder on the wall. All you have to do is climb over the wall. Someone will meet you on the other side. I don't believe this. Your face will be all over the papers tomorrow, but tonight you can do what you want.'

Twelve hours later Ray was in Mobile, Alabama.

Chapter 20   Major Trouble

On Wednesday morning Tarry Ross climbed the stairs to the fourth floor of the hotel. Vinnie Cozzo opened the door at his knock.

'Good morning, Alfred,' he said warmly. 'Would you like some coffee?'

'I didn't come here for coffee,' said Ross. 'Where's the money?'

'First you have to talk to me,' Cozzo said.

'OK. We've given McDeere a million dollars already. We paid it into a bank in the Bahamas, but he's already moved it out of there, and we don't know where. Another million is on the way. He's delivered one lot of Bendini documents and says he has ten thousand more. He's talked to our agents many times in the last six months. He'll give evidence at the trials and then disappear as a protected witness.'

'Where are the other documents?'

'He isn't saying. But he's ready to deliver them.'

As soon as Ross had left, Vinnie Cozzo called Lazarov.

Tarry Ross walked hurriedly down the hall. He had almost reached the lift when a hand reached out of nowhere and pulled him into a room. He was thrown to the floor and his briefcase full of money was emptied on to the bed.

'You disgust me, Ross,' said Voyles. 'I can't believe it's you. What did you tell Cozzo?'

Ross began to talk.

♦

DeVasher ran down the stairs to the fourth floor and burst into Locke's office. Half the partners were there and the rest were on their way.

He quickly told them what Cozzo had told Lazarov. 'The FBI have had plenty of our files for about a week already. They haven't moved. That must mean that this first lot of files is clean. McDeere was just warming them up. He's in it for the money. But we have to suppose that the next lot of files will destroy us. Where *is* McDeere?'

Milligan spoke. 'In his office. I just talked to him. He suspects nothing.'

'Good. He's due to leave in three hours for Grand Cayman, isn't he, Lambert?'

'Yes. Around midday.'

'The jet will never arrive. There'll be an explosion.'

'The jet?' asked one of the partners.

'Yeah, the jet. Don't worry, we'll buy you another toy. Lazarov is on his way. As soon as we've got rid of McDeere, we're going to look long and hard at this operation, and make whatever changes are necessary.'

Locke stood up and said to Lambert, 'Just make sure McDeere's on that jet.'

♦

Mitch's secretary picked up the phone. 'Mr McDeere's office,' she said.

'I need to speak to him,' the man's voice said.

'I'm sorry, he's busy at the moment.'

'Listen, young lady, this is Judge Henry Hugo, and he was supposed to be in my courtroom fifteen minutes ago. We're waiting for him. It's an emergency.'

'There's nothing in his diary for this morning.'

'That's your fault. Now let me speak to him.'

She ran to Mitch's office and said, 'There's a Judge Hugo on the phone. He says you're supposed to be in his court.'

Mitch jumped to his feet and grabbed the phone. He was pale. 'Yes?' he said.

'Mr McDeere,' Tarrance said. 'Judge Hugo. You're late for my court. Get over here.'

'Yes, sir.' He dropped the phone and grabbed his coat and briefcase. He was out of the office in two minutes. 'Judge Hugo' was the name Tarrance had told Mitch he would use if something went wrong and the boys on the fifth floor were after him.

He ran east for about half a mile. He made sure that no one was following him and then called Tarrance from a pay phone.

'What's happening, Tarrance?'

'Voyles just called me from Washington. One of our men has talked . . .'

'God! I knew this would happen. I knew I should never trust you! You people are inefficient fools,' Mitch shouted.

'Don't worry, Mitch. We can protect you.'

'Yeah? I've heard that before. For some funny reason I just don't trust you at the moment, Tarrance. You tell me you're going to protect me for the rest of my life, then I'm nearly gunned down in my own office! That's great! From now on, I go my own way, Tarrance.'

'What about the documents? We paid you.'

'Wrong, Tarrance. You paid me for what you've already got. Remember? Goodbye, Wayne.'

He put the phone down. At the other end Tarrance threw his phone against the wall.

Mitch had another call to make. 'Hi, Tammy,' he said when she picked up the phone.

'Hi. What's the matter?'

'Major trouble. No time to explain. I'm running and they're right behind me. Call Abby at her parents' house. Tell her to drop everything and get out. She doesn't have time to pack a suitcase. Tell her to catch a plane to Mobile. There she signs in at the Perdido Beach Hilton under the name of Rachel James.'

'OK. Anything else?'

'Yeah. Get the documents from the Doctor, then fly to Nashville and stay in the Brentwood apartment. Do not leave the phone. Then call Abanks.'

'OK. What about you?'

'I'll be coming to Nashville, but I'm not sure when. Listen, Tammy, tell Abby she could be dead within the hour if she doesn't run. Move.'

'OK, boss.'

At the airport Mitch bought several tickets in his own name for various destinations around the country. In the name of Sam Fortune, and in cash, he bought a ticket for Cincinnati.

♦

Lazarov entered the corner office on the fourth floor and no one could meet his eyes.

'We can't find him,' DeVasher said.

'You mean he just got up and walked out of here?' Lazarov asked.

There was no answer. None was needed.

'All right, DeVasher. This is the plan. Send every man you've got to the airport. Check with every airline. Where's his car?'

'In the car park.'

'He walked out of here on foot? Joey's going to love this. How many partners have we got?'

'Sixteen who are here.'

'Divide them up in pairs and send them to all the major airports in the country. Go and get his wife. Don't hurt her yet; just bring her in. Hurry!'

♦

Voyles had also come down to Memphis. At that moment he was in Tarrance's office, giving very similar instructions to his men as Lazarov was giving to his.

Chapter 21   On the Run

From Cincinnati, Mitch flew to Nashville. He hired a van and drove to the apartment. On the way he bought some equipment from a photography shop.

When he arrived Tammy gave him some food. At ten he called the Perdido Hilton. He asked for Rachel James, but she hadn't arrived. He asked for Lee Stevens. After a few moments someone picked up the phone.

'Yeah?'

'This is Mitch. Congratulations.'

Ray fell on the bed and closed his eyes. 'It was so easy, Mitch. How did you do it?'

'I'll tell you when we have time. But at the moment there are a lot of people trying to kill Abby and me. We're on the run. Don't ask me about it now. It's the Mafia and the FBI.'

'Is that all?'

Mitch laughed. 'Abby will be arriving at your hotel soon. Check that she isn't being followed, OK? She's calling herself Rachel James.' He gave Ray the number of the Brentwood apartment. 'Remember that number, Ray. If I'm not here, someone called Tammy will be. You can trust her. Take care of my wife and call me when she gets there.'

'OK, Mitch. And thanks.'

♦

Abby arrived an hour later in a hired car. She parked and walked towards the front door of the hotel. She stopped for a second and looked behind her.

Two minutes later a yellow taxi from Mobile also parked. Ray watched the taxi. A woman got out of the back and walked into the hotel. Ray followed her.

The woman approached the counter and asked for a room.

Then she said, 'What's the name of that lady who just signed in here? She seemed familiar. I think she's an old friend.'

The clerk looked through his cards. 'Rachel James,' he said.

'Yeah, that's her. What room is she in? I'd like to say hello.'

'I can't give room numbers,' said the clerk.

The woman pulled two twenties from her purse and slid them across the counter. 'I only want to say hello.'

The clerk took the money. 'Room 622.'

'Where are the phones?' the woman asked.

'Around the corner,' said the clerk, and pointed.

Ray got there first. He grabbed a phone and pretended to be talking to someone. He heard only a few words of the woman's conversation: '... Mobile ... Room 622 ... send some help ... an hour? OK.'

Ten minutes later there was a knock at the door of her room. The woman jumped up from the bed, grabbed her gun and stuck it into her trousers under her shirt. She cautiously opened the door.

Ray burst in and knocked her against the wall. He jumped at her, took her gun and pinned her to the floor. With her face in the carpet, he pushed the gun into her ear. 'If you move or make a sound,' he said, 'I'll kill you.'

He opened her suitcase. 'Open your mouth,' he said, and pushed a pair of socks in. He tied her up tightly with clothes from her case and slid her under the bed. Then he left with her gun.

♦

The phone went at 1 a.m., and Mitch was not asleep. He was studying documents.

'Hello,' he answered cautiously.

'It's Ray.'

'Where are you, Ray? I can hear music.'

'In a bar. We had to move out of the hotel; Abby was followed.'

'Abby's there? She's safe?'

62

*Ray burst in and knocked her against the wall. He jumped at her,
took her gun and pinned her to the floor.*

'Yeah. Now what?'

'Drive to Panama City Beach and get two rooms at the Holiday Hotel. Call me when you're there.'

'I hope you know what you're doing.'

'Trust me, Ray.'

'I do, but I'm beginning to wish I was back in prison.'

'You can't go back, Ray. We either disappear or we're dead.'

Chapter 22   The Hunt Gets Closer

The taxi stopped in the middle of Nashville and Mitch got out. He entered the Southeastern Bank Building and asked to see Mr Laycook. He had learned a lot over the last few weeks. He knew all the right dates and numbers to pass the bank's tests. They let him wire ten million dollars out of the Royal Bank of Montreal in Grand Cayman into their bank. As soon as it arrived he moved a million to his mother's bank, a million to Abby's parents' bank and a million for Tammy. The other seven million joined what was left of the FBI money in his bank in Zurich.

On the top floor of the Royal Bank of Montreal in Grand Cayman, Randolph Osgood was informed, as was proper, of the movement of a large amount of money. He picked up the phone and called Memphis. A receptionist told him that Mr Tolleson was not available. Then Nathan Locke? he asked. Mr Locke is out of town. Victor Milligan? Mr Milligan is away too.

Osgood decided to try again tomorrow.

♦

Next day the hunt got closer. The police were looking for a man who had attacked a woman in the Perdido Beach Hilton. When Ray McDeere's picture appeared in the papers as an escaped murderer, the hotel clerk connected him with the attack and told the police that he was with a woman called Rachel James. The victim of the attack, Karen Adair, supported by her boyfriend Aaron Rimmer, agreed that the criminal was Ray McDeere. Then the clerk remembered that Rachel James was driving a white Cutlass. The police began to search for the car.

◆

It took seventeen trips from the apartment to the van with all the boxes. Then Mitch sat in the apartment and wrote down instructions for Tammy. He also told her that there was a million dollars waiting for her in her bank.

He spoke to Abby at the Holiday Hotel in Panama City Beach. She told him about the police hunt for Ray, which was in all the newspapers.

'Where's Ray now?'

'On the beach, trying to brown his face. I've told him everything. He's also had a haircut.'

'Good idea. Abby, you must cut your hair and colour it blonde. But first you must get out of there. Just walk out. Make it look as if you're going for a walk on the beach. But a mile east along the beach is a small hotel called the Blue Tide. Sign in there as Jackie Nagel. I'll be there soon. Don't worry; there are so many hotels and buildings along the beach there that it'll take them a year to search them all.'

Twelve hours later the three of them were together.

Chapter 23   Panama City Beach

Joey Morolto flew down with forty of his men. He settled himself in the Sandpiper Hotel. The first thing he did was get all the available partners and associates from Memphis to come to Alabama. These people knew McDeere; they could recognize him.

Three miles along the beach, F. Denton Voyles and Tarrance were sitting in *their* hotel, waiting for news. They had sixty FBI agents and hundreds of local cops searching for the car.

The white Cutlass was found at nine in the morning in the car park of an apartment building in Panama City Beach. Voyles immediately moved all his men down there.

A local cop phoned that nice Mr Rimmer to tell him the news, so that he and his pretty girlfriend would feel better. Mr Rimmer called Lazarov at the Sandpiper. Rimmer and Lazarov immediately moved all their men down to Panama City Beach.

♦

It took only a few minutes for the van to become hot news. The man who had rented it to Mitch was reading his morning paper and he remembered the name 'McDeere'. He looked through his records and phoned the police. A short while later Voyles and Tarrance got the news. They realized that the van must be for carrying the files.

♦

At nine, Mitch called Tammy. She had the new documents and passports. Mitch told her to send them to Sam Fortune at the Blue Tide Hotel and gave her the address. He told her to make sure they arrived the next day. Finally he told her to leave Nashville, drive to Knoxville and call him from there.

By midday, all the roads to the coast around Panama City Beach were closed by the police. Lazarov and Morolto were in the Best Western Hotel, while their men were out searching.

At four in the afternoon, a clerk in the Holiday Hotel told the police that Abby McDeere was probably the woman who had paid cash for two rooms for three nights but hadn't really used either of them.

At 4.58, a police car stopped in the car park of a cheap hotel and found the van Mitch had rented. It was empty.

♦

Andy Patrick had first gone to prison, for four months, when he was nineteen. Since then he had committed plenty of minor crimes. He hated violence. He hated cops. A cop had once beaten him so badly that he lost one eye.

Six months ago he found himself in Panama City Beach and got a job as a clerk at the Blue Tide Hotel. Around nine on Friday night he was watching TV when the cop walked in.

'We're looking for some people,' said the cop, and laid pictures on the counter. 'Seen any of them?'

Andy studied the pictures. He thought he recognized the one of Mitchell Y. McDeere. His criminal's mind began to work.

'I haven't seen them,' he said. 'I'll tell you if I do.'

'They're dangerous,' said the cop.

You're the dangerous one, Andy thought.

As soon as the cop had left, Andy went and knocked on the door of Room 38. He could see the red lights of police cars passing on the road behind the hotel.

'Who's there?' a woman's voice said.

'The manager,' Andy replied.

Mitch opened the door. Andy could see he was nervous. 'What is it?' he asked.

'The police were just here,' Andy explained. 'They showed me some pictures. I said I couldn't recognize them. Do you know what I mean? They said one of these people had been in prison. I've been in prison too, and I think everyone should escape. Am I making myself clear?'

'Yes,' Mitch said. 'What's your name?'

'Andy.'

'Andy, I'll give you a thousand dollars now, and another thousand tomorrow, if you're still unable to recognize any of the faces in the pictures.'

'Five thousand a day,' Andy said.

'OK. And I'll give you another five thousand to bring me a small packet that will arrive tomorrow morning.'

'Good.' Andy went back to his counter.

Back in the room, Mitch said, 'I think our luck has just changed for the better.'

Chapter 24   On the Floor Among the Boxes

'Why here?' Lazarov asked. 'Why did they choose Panama City Beach? They're trapped here. The cops have got the whole place covered. There are only about sixty of our men, and the cops have got hundreds. So the chances are that they'll find them before we do.'

Morolto nodded. 'So we've got to improve our chances.'

'Leave that to me,' DeVasher said. 'But why here? It's good for them that there are a lot of small hotels, but we can still send our people to search them, room by room. It'll take time, but we can do it.'

'The water!' Morolto suddenly shouted. 'They're going to try to escape by sea, in the dark!'

'That makes sense to me,' DeVasher said.

'So where are our boats?' Morolto said.

Lazarov jumped from his seat and began shouting orders down the phone. He wanted his men to hire every available boat and stay out at sea, waiting.

DeVasher gave his own orders to Rimmer and his men. Rimmer drove up to Tallahassee and phoned the police from there. 'Listen!' he said excitedly. 'I just saw those three people you're after. They're driving a green Ford van! They're going south!'

Five minutes later Fat Tony Verkler did exactly the same from a few miles further south.

Within a couple of hours nearly all the local cops had returned to their stations, and all the FBI agents were travelling south.

◆

Mitch, Abby and Ray watched the news on TV. Now that the police search had moved away from Panama City Beach it was more dangerous for them. The police only wanted to arrest them; Morolto's men wanted to kill them.

Early the next morning Mitch sat back down on the floor among all the boxes. He nodded at Abby, who was operating the camera. He continued giving evidence. After sixteen hours he had nearly finished. With the help of Tammy's lists he told the court where they could find nine hundred million dollars of Mafia money in banks. He then explained how the whole system worked and who the most important figures were. For six hours he explained the various methods the Moroltos and their lawyers used to turn dirty money into clean. He knew that the evidence was incomplete, but when the FBI had these films they could easily get permission to search the whole Bendini Building and all its computer records.

◆

At 10.35 Andy Patrick received the envelope addressed to Sam Fortune. He started to take it over to Room 38 but stopped when he saw two men knocking at the doors to the rooms. He went back to the reception desk and phoned Room 38.

'Mr Fortune? I think you should know there are two men coming your way. They're knocking on all the doors.'

'Are they cops?'

'I don't think so. They didn't come and see me first.'

'Thanks. We'll switch the lights off and not answer the door. They'll think the room's empty. What about the packet?'

'It's here.'

'OK. Can you bring it over as soon as it's safe?'

'Yeah.'

♦

In Room 38 they admired the new documents and passports. The Doctor certainly knew his work.

'We have to celebrate,' Ray said. 'Besides, I'm going crazy in here. I'm going to get us some beers.'

'Ray, no,' Mitch said. 'There's no need to take chances.'

But Ray wasn't listening. He stayed close to the walls until he reached the end of the hotel. There was a row of shops next to the hotel. He waited until he was sure no one was looking and then went into the supermarket.

In the car park in front of the shops Lamar Quin saw Ray enter the shop. The way the man moved was familiar. He walked over to the shop and went inside. He took a Coke and waited to pay for it until he came face to face with the man. It wasn't Mitch McDeere, but he looked just like him.

It was Ray. It had to be. The face was darker than his prison photograph, and he was wearing sunglasses, but this was definitely a McDeere.

'How's it going?' Lamar said to the man.

'Fine. You?' Even the voice was similar.

Lamar paid for his drink and returned to the car park. He calmly put the Coke in his car. Then he went to the next shop to continue his search for the McDeeres.

Chapter 25   The Pier

The Dan Russell Pier was the one which was furthest west of the three piers on Panama City Beach. It was about half a mile east of the Blue Tide. At eleven-thirty Abby left Room 38 and began walking east along the beach. Five minutes later Mitch left. While Abby was dressed to look like a tourist, Mitch was dressed all in black. So was Ray, who left five minutes after Mitch, locking the door behind him.

At midnight Abby stood at the end of the pier. Mitch sat on a chair at the beach end of the pier. Ray was standing on the sand about fifty yards away.

Abby hid as much of her torch as possible in her coat and pointed it out to sea. She switched it on and off, on and off. There was no reply. She tried again. Again there was no reply.

From the corner of his eye Mitch saw someone jump on to the pier and walk quickly towards Abby. It was Rimmer. Mitch was up and running silently after him.

Rimmer walked up behind Abby and called her name. She turned round and started to scream. Rimmer jumped at her and at the same time Mitch dived head first into his legs. All three fell down on to the hard surface of the pier. Rimmer hit Mitch hard in the eye and reached for his gun. He never found it. Ray charged into him and hit him again and again until he was unconscious.

'Switch on the torch again, Abby,' Ray said as he unwrapped the rope from his waist. She turned out to sea and did as he said.

'What are you going to do?' Mitch whispered, watching Ray and the rope.

'We can either shoot him or drown him,' Ray said. 'We have to do one or the other.'

'Oh, my God!' said Abby.

'Don't fire the gun,' Mitch whispered.

'I agree,' Ray said. He twisted the rope around Rimmer's neck and tightened it. Rimmer didn't move. After three minutes Ray slid the body at the end of the rope down into the water.

Abanks was late, but he found a way through the small boats

Ray twisted the rope aroung Rimmer's neck and tightened it.
Rimmer didn't move.

which were waiting out at sea. None of Morolto's men even saw him come, and none of them saw him go with his three new passengers.

◆

At six in the morning Tammy phoned Tarrance, just as Mitch had said she should.

'You can have the files now, Wayne,' she said. 'They're in Room 38, Blue Tide Hotel, Panama City Beach. The clerk is called Andy and he'll let you into the room. Be careful with the files, Wayne, we've taken a lot of time and trouble getting them all neat for you. And you'll find sixteen hours of film there too.'

'I have just one question,' Tarrance said tiredly. 'Where is he?'

'By now,' said Tammy, 'they're on a plane to South America. I've got to go. Goodbye.'

◆

The boat Abanks had bought them was perfect. With it and the money they could spend the rest of their lives sailing in luxury among the thousands of islands in the West Indies. They could have homes on two or three of the smaller ones, like Little Cayman, where no one ever came. Abanks taught them all he knew about boating and about the islands.

They knew from newspapers that the firm and the Morolto family were finished. Fifty-one present and past members of the firm were arrested, and the Morolto family trials would go on for years. The Memphis newspapers listed the names of all the arrested lawyers. As Mitch read their names he saw their faces. He almost felt sorry for some of them, and he pitied their wives and children. What a waste of talent.

'I love you, Mitch.' Abby was standing behind him. 'We'll be OK. As long as we're together we can handle anything.'

'I never really wanted to be a lawyer, anyway,' Mitch said. 'I always wanted to be a sailor.'

ACTIVITIES

Chapters 1–5

Before you read

1 Look at the Word List at the back of the book and then answer these questions.

   a Which six words refer to people or groups of people?

   b Do *cops* normally wear a *badge* or a *bikini*?

2 Read the Introduction to this book and answer these questions. What do you learn about:

   a the Cayman Islands?

   b the similarities between Mitchell McDeere's life and John Grisham's?

3 Look at the titles of the chapters. In which chapter(s) will you read about.

   a how the firm operates?

   b important places in the story?

   c important characters in the story?

While you read

4 Match the names with the descriptions.

   a Mitchell McDeere   .....

   b Abby McDeere   .....

   c Ray McDeere   .....

   d Lamar Quin   .....

   e DeVasher   .....

   f Oliver Lambert   .....

   g Kozinski   .....

   h Tarrance   .....

   i Hodge   .....

   j Lazarov   .....

   1) Mitchell's beautiful wife

   2) worries because the firm can not find Mitch's brother

   3) a twenty-five-year-old graduate of Harvard Law School

   4) an FBI agent

5) is working with Kozinski

6) head of security in Bendini, Lambert and Locke

7) Mitchell's brother

8) the FBI finds the firm's bugs in his house

9) is one of the firm's bosses in Chicago

10) an associate in Bendini, Lambert and Locke

After you read

5 Discuss these questions. What do you know about the relationship between these people?

   a the firm's partners and associates

   b the McDeeres and the Quins

   c Marty Kozinski and Joe Hodge

   d Avery Tolleson and Mitch McDeere

   e DeVasher and Lazarov

6 What are the firm's feelings or rules about its members':

   a marriages and family life?

   b holidays?

   c drinking?

   d privacy?

   e meetings with the FBI?

7 What do you know about:

   a Mitch's ambitious goals?

   b Abby's feelings about Mitch's work?

   c Ray McDeere's past?

Chapters 6–9

Before you read

8 What do you think the firm wants to keep secret? What kind of work might they do? Why do they want to bug their associates' houses? Is there anything strange about the deaths of Kozinski and Hodge?

9 Read the titles of Chapters 6–9 and look at the picture on page 15. How is Mitch's life going to change, do you think?

While you read

10 What do two men do while the McDeeres are having dinner at Justine's? Put a (✓) next to the correct answers.

   a They take Lambert's BMW to the McDeeres' house.   .....

   b They put microphones into the mouthpiece of each phone.   .....

   c They put microphones in each room.   .....

   d They connect all the microphones to a receiver.   .....

   e They eat fish with the McDeeres.   .....

   f They listen to the McDeeres in their bedroom.   .....

11 Five lawyers from the firm have died in the past fifteen years. How did they die? Draw a line from the names to the way they died.

   a Alice Knauss   a bullet in his head

   b Robert Lamm   explosion on a boat

   c John Mickel   car crash

   d Marty Kozinski   shot himself

   e Joe Hodge   explosion on a boat

12 Write the correct name. Who:

   a is a private investigator?   ....

   b is a sexy secretary?   ....

   c goes to Rumheads and drinks heavily?   ....

   d has sex with a woman on the beach?   ....

After you read

13 What does Mitch hear about Kozinski and Hodge's deaths from:

   a Wayne Tarrance?

   b Nathan Locke?

   c Barry Abanks?

14 Who says this and why? Who are they talking to?

   a 'Money doesn't grow on trees.'

   b 'He's dangerous. You are not to speak to him again.'

   c 'Now you are ours. Now you'll do anything for us.'

Chapters 10–13

Before you read

15 What do you think Mitch suspects is happening at the firm?

16 Look at the pictures on pages 27 and 35. Who is Mitch talking to and what do you think they are talking about?

While you read

17 Put these events in the correct order. Write 1–6.

    a Mitch tells Abby about Tarrance, the firm's bugs, and
       the five dead lawyers. .....

    b Lomax gives Mitch information about the three dead
       lawyers. .....

    c Mitch meets the boss of the FBI, Denton Voyles. .....

    d Tammy meets Mitch and they promise to keep in touch. .....

    e Eddie Lomax is shot in a car park. .....

    f Mitch learns that the firm is owned by the Morolto
       Mafia family. .....

18 What happens to Mitch next? Put a (✓) next to the correct sentences.

    a Voyles asks Mitch to photocopy the firm's files and
       bank records for the FBI. .....

    b Tarrance takes Mitch to a shoe shop to buy shoes. .....

    c DeVasher shows Mitch photos of him on the beach
       with the woman. .....

    d Mitch shouts at DeVasher angrily. .....

After you read

19 What do you know about:

    a the deaths of the three lawyers?

    b the owners of the firm and the way the firm operates?

20 Work with another student and have this conversation.

    Student A: You are Mitch and you are in a bar with your wife. Tell Abby about Eddie Lomax and the five dead lawyers. Tell her everything you know and what you suspect.

Student B: You are Abby. You and Mitch are sitting in the bar. He is telling you some very shocking news about his job. Listen, ask questions, and make suggestions.

Chapters 14–17

Before you read

21 What do you think Mitch will decide to do? Will he help the FBI? If he does, how will his and Abby's lives change?

22 Read the titles of Chapters 14–16. What will be in the two black briefcases? Look at the picture on page 46. What is the woman doing? Why?

While you read

23 Circle the correct words to complete the sentences.

   a Tammy rents an office on the ninth floor; Mulholland's office is on … .

     1) the fifth. **2)** the fourth. **3)** the seventh.

   b Tammy gets in the lift with exactly the same kind of … .

     1) bag. **2)** briefcase. **3)** signal.

   c Tammy gets nine more files to copy from … .

     1) Mitch's Volkswagen. **2)** Abby's Peugeot. **3)** the school.

   d Mitch wants the FBI to pay him … dollars.

     1) one million. **2)** two million. **3)** three million.

   e Mitch also wants the FBI to get Ray … .

     1) out of prison. **2)** a million dollars. **3)** a good lawyer.

24 Which person does these things? Write A for Abby and T for Tammy.

   a She goes to the Bendini Building unexpectedly.   .....

   b She tells Mitch that her mother is ill.   .....

   c She leaves Memphis and flies to Nashville.   .....

   d She meets Avery Tolleson and gets him drunk.   .....

   e She puts sleeping powder in Tolleson's drink.   .....

   f She rents a photocopier to copy Tolleson's files.   .....

g She gets copies of Tolleson's keys.   .....

h She gets into bed with Tolleson just before he wakes up. .....

i She flies in and out of the Caymans, taking papers to
Brentwood.   .....

j She tells Tarrance he can see a couple files when Ray
is out of prison.   .....

After you read

25 Who are the speakers talking to and what do they mean?

    a 'Midday tomorrow?' asks Tammy.

    b 'If you can't do it by bending the rules, then you can help him
escape,' says Mitch.

    c 'We need some time away from each other. I think it will be
good for both of us,' says Abby.

    d 'She's our best lever!' says DeVasher.

    e 'He couldn't do it if he had to,' says Tammy.

26 Discuss these questions about Tarry Ross.

    a Who does he work for?

    b Which Mafia family does he work for?

    c What does he know about Mitchell McDeere?

    d How much money will Vinnie Cozzo pay him for information
about Mitch?

Chapters 18–20

Before you read

27 Say what you think about these questions.

    a Will Tarry Ross give information about Mitch to Vinnie Cozzo?

    b Will Mitch, Abby and Tammy get caught?

    c Will the Mafia get to Mitch before he gives the files to the
FBI?

28 What will the FBI do about Ray, do you think? Is Mitch wise to
make Ray's freedom a condition for handing over the files?

While you read

29 Are these sentences True or False? Write T or F.

   a McDeere makes two thousand photocopies at 3 a.m..   .....

   b McDeere's secretary uses the same eighteen file numbers to make another two thousand copies.   .....

   c DeVasher suspects that somebody on Grand Cayman made copies of Avery's keys.   .....

   d The FBI arrange for Ray to escape from Prison.   .....

   e Voyles catches Ross after he gives Cozzo information about Mitch.   .....

   f DeVasher plans to kill hundreds of passengers on the jet to Grand Cayman.   .....

   g 'Judge Hugo' warns Mitch that something is wrong.   .....

   h Tammy goes to a hotel in Mobile.   .....

   i Lazarov sends sixteen partners airports to find Mitch.   .....

   j Lazarov tells DeVasher to kill Abby.   .....

After you read

30 Who are these people? Why are they or their names important?

   a Aaron Rimmer

   b Victor Milligan

   c the Doctor

   d Alfred

   e Judge Hugo

   f Rachel James

   g Sam Fortune

31 Do you think that DeVasher is very clever? Why (not)?

Chapters 21–25

Before you read

32 Abby is on her way to Mobile, Alabama and Tammy is going to the Brentwood apartment in Nashville, Tennessee. Mitch has bought a ticket to Cincinnati, Ohio. What will they do next and where do you think they will meet? How will Abanks help them?

33 Read the titles of Chapters 21–25 and look at the pictures on pages 63 and 72. What do you think will happen?

34 Write the missing name or word in each sentence.

    a Mitch flies to .... and drives to the Brentwood apartment.

    b .... attacks the woman who followed Abby.

    c The police are searching for ....'s white Cutlass.

    d Abby cuts and colours her hair and changes her name to ....

    e .... and forty men from the firm fly to Mobile, Alabama.

    f Sixty .... and hundreds of cops are searching for the white Cutlass car.

    g The police find ....'s rented van.

    h .... has offered to help Mitch for five thousand dollars a day.

    i Karen Adair, girlfriend of ...., says Ray McDeere attacked her.

    j .... films Mitch giving evidence to be used in court against the Mafia.

After you read

35 How do these people help Mitch?

    a Andy Patrick

    b the Doctor

    c Abanks

    d Tammy

Writing

36 Imagine you are Beth Kozinski. Write a letter to Oliver Lambert, who is now in prison. Tell him what you think of him and of the lies he told after your husband's death.

37 Mitch's desire for wealth brought him into contact with the Mafia. He risked his life, and his wife's, for justice. Write about his life for a magazine.

38 Write a conversation between Mitch and Ray when Mitch tells Ray about Eddie Lomax's help and then his death.

39 Write a conversation between Wayne Tarrance and Denton Voyles just after they see the files for the first time and the film of Mitch giving evidence.

40 Imagine you are Abby. Choose one day from the story and write about it in your diary. Write what happened and how you felt.

41 Imagine you work for a Memphis newspaper. Write a report on the surveillance equipment found on the fifth floor of the Bendini Building just after the arrest of the partners and lawyers.

42 Find out more about the FBI. Do you think that they do a good job? Why (not)?

43 Write a letter to John Grisham and tell him what you thought about this book, and which part you liked best and why.

44 Which character do you think was most helpful to Mitch? Write about that character and his/her actions.

45 It is two years after the end of this story. Write another chapter. Write what you think has happened to Mitch, Abby and Ray.

WORD LIST

agent (n) a person who works for a government or police department; a person who represents another person or company

armed (adj) carrying weapons, especially a gun

arrest (v/n) to take someone, with force if necessary, to a police station because they are suspected of a crime

associate (n) someone who you work or do business with

badge (n) a small piece of metal or plastic that you carry to show that you work for an organization, such as the police

bikini (n) a piece of clothing in two separate parts that women wear for swimming

briefcase (n) a small case used especially by business people for carrying documents

client (n) someone who receives a service from a professional person or organization

cop (n) a police officer (informal)

determined (adj) having a strong desire to do something, and not let anyone stop you

evidence (n) facts that show clearly that something exists or is true

firm (n) a company

grab (v) to take hold of something with a sudden or violent movement

grin (n) a wide smile

investigate (v) to try to find out the truth about something

legend (n) someone who is famous and admired for being extremely good at doing something

luxury (n) very great comfort and pleasure, usually expensive

Mafia (n) a large organized group of criminals who control many illegal activities, especially in Italy and the US

major (adj) large or important

minor (adj) small or unimportant

negotiate (v) to discuss something and reach an agreement

nod (v) to move your head up and down to mean 'Yes'

pier (n) a walkway that is built over water so that boats can stop next to it or people can walk along it

rely on (v) to trust or depend on

ridiculous (adj) very silly or unreasonable

security (n) protection from danger and crime

surveillance (n) the careful watching of a person or place

tempt (v) to try to persuade someone to do something by making it seem attractive

victim (n) someone who has been attacked

visible (adj) able to be seen

A Time to Kill
John Grisham

Ten-year-old Tonya Hailey is attacked and raped by two local men.
Carl Lee, Tonya's father, shoots them. Now only his lawyer and
friend, Jake Brigance, stands between him and the electric chair.
Is there a legal defense for Carl Lee's actions?

The Rainmaker
John Grisham

*I have no job. I have no money. I have debts I can't pay. I do,
however, have a case.*

Rudy Baylor is ready to finish law school but loses his first job
before he has even started. Then Dot and Bud Black ask for his
help in their fight against a powerful insurance company. Their son,
Donny Ray, is dying. His claim for medical insurance has been
refused. Can Rudy, an inexperienced student, really give them any
hope?

The Pelican Brief
John Grisham

In Washington, two Supreme Court judges are murdered and only
the young and beautiful law student Darby Shaw knows why. She
has uncovered a deadly secret but will anyone believe her? Can
she stay alive long enough to persuade them she is right?

*There are hundreds of Penguin Readers to choose from – world classics,
film adaptations, modern-day crime and adventure, short stories,
biographies, American classics, non-fiction, plays ...*

For a complete list of all Penguin Readers titles, please contact your local
Pearson Longman office or visit our website.

www.penguinreaders.com

Longman Dictionaries

Express yourself with confidence!

*Longman has led the way in ELT dictionaries since 1935.
We constantly talk to students and teachers around the
world to find out what they need from a learner's dictionary.*

Why choose a Longman dictionary?

Easy to understand

Longman invented the Defining Vocabulary – 2000 of the most
common words which are used to write the definitions in our
dictionaries. So Longman definitions are always clear and easy
to understand.

Real, natural English

All Longman dictionaries contain natural examples taken from
real-life that help explain the meaning of a word and show you
how to use it in context.

Avoid common mistakes

Longman dictionaries are written specially for learners, and we
make sure that you get all the help you need to avoid common
mistakes. We analyse typical learners' mistakes and include
notes on how to avoid them.

Innovative CD-ROMs

Longman are leaders in dictionary CD-ROM innovation. Did
you know that a dictionary CD-ROM includes features to help
improve your pronunciation, help you practice for exams and
improve your writing skills?

**For details of all Longman dictionaries, and to choose
the one that's right for you, visit our website:**

www.longman.com/dictionaries